Phonics Handbook

Complete teaching and assessment support

Authors: Emily Guille-Marrett and Charlotte Raby

- Lilac
- Pink A
- Pink B
- Red A
- Red B
- Yellow

Collins

William Collins' dream of knowledge for all began with the publication of his first book in 1819.

A self-educated mill worker, he not only enriched millions of lives, but also founded a flourishing publishing house. Today, staying true to this spirit, Collins books are packed with inspiration, innovation and practical expertise. They place you at the centre of a world of possibility and give you exactly what you need to explore it.

Collins. Freedom to teach.

An imprint of HarperCollins*Publishers*
The News Building
1 London Bridge Street
London
SE1 9GF

Browse the complete Collins catalogue at
www.collins.co.uk

© HarperCollins*Publishers* Limited 2018

10 9 8 7 6 5 4 3 2

ISBN 978-0-00-826421-5

All rights reserved. No part of this publication may be reproduced, stored in a retrieval system, or transmitted in any form by any means, electronic, mechanical, photocopying, recording or otherwise, without the prior written permission of the Publisher or a licence permitting restricted copying in the United Kingdom issued by the Copyright Licensing Agency Ltd., Barnard's Inn, 86 Fetter Lane, London, EC4A 1EN.

British Library Cataloguing in Publication Data
A catalogue record for this publication is available from the British Library.

Authors: Charlotte Raby and Emily Guille-Marrett

Commissioning editor: Sarah Thomas

In-house editor: Caroline Green

Development editor: Helen Lewis

Project managers: Tracy Thomas and Emily Hooton

Copyeditor: Tanya Solomons

Proofreader: Karen Williams

Cover design: 2hoots Publishing Services Ltd

Cover artwork: Alex Paterson (Plum Pudding Agency)

Typesetter: 2hoots Publishing Services Ltd

Artwork: **Beehive illustration:** Matt Ward, Beatrice Bencivenni, Rosie Brooks, Judy Brown, Keri Green, Davide Ortu, Deborah Partington, Angeles Peinador, Laszlo Veres; **Advocate Art:** Monica Armino, Beatriz Castro, Estelle Corke, Amanda Enright, Laura Gonazalez, Susana Gurrea, Erin Taylor; **Sylvie Poggio Artists:** Beccy Blake, Andy Elkerton; **Plum Pudding Agency:** Alex Paterson; **The Bright Agency:** Benedetta Capriotti; Laura Hambleton; Julian Mosedale.

Photographs: p113 Will Amlot Photography © HarperCollins Publishers, p116 bl Eric Isselee/Shutterstock, p143 bl Wilm Ihlenfeld/Shutterstock, p160 t Will Amlot Photography © HarperCollins Publishers.

Production controller: Sarah Burke

Printed and bound by CPI Group (UK) Ltd, Croydon, CR0 4YY

Contents

Introduction	4
Using Letters and Sounds	6
Curriculum coverage	8
The Phonics Screening Check	11
The *Big Cat Phonics for Letters and Sounds* view of reading	12
Starting the reading journey with *Big Cat Phonics for Letters and Sounds*	14
Becoming a reading school	16
Big Cat Phonics for Letters and Sounds chart	18
Teaching common exception words with *Big Cat Phonics for Letters and Sounds*	22
Fluency in reading	24
Big Cat Phonics assessment	25
Support for Lilac books Introduction	36
Number Fun	38
I Spy Nursery Rhymes	43
I Spy Fairytales	48
Animal Fun	53
Sound Walk	58
My Day, Our World	63
Support for Pink books Introduction	68
How to teach a new sound	70
What to teach while reading Pink books	71
Pat it (Chant and Chatter Book 1)	72
Pit Pat (Chant and Chatter Book 2)	75
Sip it (Chant and Chatter Book 3)	78
Map Man (Chant and Chatter Book 4)	81
Pip Pip Pip (Chant and Chatter Book 5)	84
Tip it (Chant and Chatter Book 6)	87
Dig it (Chant and Chatter Book 7)	90
Not a Pot (Chant and Chatter Book 8)	93
Pop Pop Pop! (Chant and Chatter Book 9)	96
Up on Deck (Chant and Chatter Book 10)	99
Mog and Mim (Chant and Chatter Book 11)	102
Bad Luck, Dad (Chant and Chatter Book 12)	105
Support for Red books Introduction	108
What to teach while reading Red books	109
This is My Kit	111
Zip and Zigzag	114
Big Mud Run	117
Fantastic Yak	120
In the Fish Tank	123
Up in a Rocket	126
Pink Boat, Pink Car	129
A Bee on a Lark	132
Wow Cow!	135
Get Set For Fun	138
It is Hidden	141
Look at Them Go	144
Support for Yellow books Introduction	147
What to teach while reading Yellow books	148
The Best Vest Quest	149
From the Top	152
In the Frog Bog	155
Stunt Jets	158
The Foolish, Timid Rabbit	161
How the Ear Can Hear	164
Letters and Sounds grapheme charts	167
Common exception words	169
Focus phonemes in each Pink A – Red A book	170
Reading for pleasure books	171
Nursery Rhymes booklet	174

© HarperCollins*Publishers* 2018

Introduction

Dear Teacher,

We are delighted to be able to share the Collins *Big Cat Phonics for Letters and Sounds* series with you and your children. Our belief is that for children to be fluent, engaged readers who understand, enjoy and learn from books, we need to see reading as a series of interconnected and orchestrated skills. The *Big Cat Phonics for Letters and Sounds* series of fiction and non-fiction books has been developed to help you do just that – supporting a foundation for early reading success and a culture of reading for pleasure.

From phonics to fluency and fun

Big Cat Phonics for Letters and Sounds has been created to support your phonics teaching and learning in the classroom, helping children move from decoding words to reading fluently and for pleasure. The books are fully linked to the Primary *National Strategy* Letters and Sounds: Principles and Practice of High Quality Phonics, and are underpinned by the latest research and best practice. The handbooks offer lesson plans, practical tips, further reading suggestions for you and your children and linked photocopiable resource sheets throughout.

Engaging picture books to inspire and provoke curiosity

It has been a real privilege to work on the much-loved Collins Big Cat series. With so many talented authors, illustrators, photographers and industry experts wanting to collaborate on the series it has allowed us to work with a great team to design a range of engaging fiction and non-fiction books – producing books that children want to read. We have worked with the Big Cat team at Collins Learning to find a variety of subject matters and artwork styles to appeal to the most discerning of little readers.

Rigorous phonics progression for early reading success

We know that if children practise reading decodable books at the right level (at 90% fluency) they experience reading success from the outset. All our books are underpinned by rigorous phonics progression to build readers' confidence. The series begins with wordless books linked to nursery rhymes and environmental sounds (Phase 1 of Letters and Sounds). Children then practise their first letters and sounds in the Collins *Big Cat Chant and Chatter* range through fun stories and fact books, before practising a progressive range of graphemes in early chapter books up to book band Turquoise (Phases 5–6).

We have embedded assessment throughout the teaching notes inside the books and in the handbooks to help you gauge where each child is on their personal reading journey. This is then followed up with advice for next steps, which includes comprehension and common exception word recognition support, as well as phonics.

A rich vocabulary for reading fluency and long-term success

Research shows that children need a vocabulary of 20,000 words to be able to read the canon of children's literature fluently. The *Big Cat Phonics for Letters and Sounds* series begins with quality wordless books created by us to support Phase 1 of Letters and Sounds, encouraging children to talk, develop a rich vocabulary and build a strong foundation for learning to read.

We believe phonics doesn't mean children cannot be exposed to a rich and challenging vocabulary. We have challenged our authors, editors and ourselves to utilise a rich vocabulary at the right level, in the appropriate context and without affecting the flow of a good read. That's why you will find words such as 'fantastic' and 'habitat' in many of the early books.

You will also find opportunities to explore vocabulary further in the activity resource sheets that accompany each book.

Reading for pleasure embedded throughout

Reading is more than just decoding words on a page. We know that phonics is critical, but at its heart reading is a creative process. This is what is special about the Collins *Big Cat Phonics for Letters and Sounds* series of books and teaching support.

The *Big Cat Phonics for Letters and Sounds* series promotes children as the 'boss of a book' – we want children to see themselves as readers from the very beginning. If children can read wordless books then they are getting a direct sense that their experiences and ideas are part of the reading process.

We also know that children need to be read a rich diet of stories and non-fiction books to experience reading for pleasure. Books that are created for learning to read cannot do this alone. And we are asking teachers to find ways of ensuring children are read to regularly. That is why we have included a list of quality children's literature and non-fiction books that are linked to the themes in each Collins Big Cat title to widen a child's reading experience and enhance their enjoyment of the book they are reading themselves. This list is by no means exhaustive and we have also included links to additional ideas and resources for building a culture of reading for pleasure in your classroom.

Supporting your Continued Professional Development

Big Cat Phonics for Letters and Sounds is informed by educational research, the best teaching practice and our own ongoing research in the reading community.

We know that the best teaching and learning should be informed by educational research. We have referenced the most up to date academic and government papers throughout this teaching handbook. If you want to take your CPD further, or just want to find out more, the full citation of each academic article or suggested resource is referenced.

Building a community of educators and readers

We are committed to supporting people and organisations who want to give children the best start for reading for life. Through the Big Cat team at Collins Learning, to accompany the *Big Cat for Letters and Sounds* series, we have created a range of videos and online support – please visit collins.co.uk for more information and to keep up to date with events. You can also connect with us on Twitter @EmilyEatsBooks and @CharlotteRaby.

We hope you enjoy using the Collins *Big Cat Phonics for Letters and Sounds* series in your classroom as much as we have enjoyed working with the team to create it. Together, we can all work to help every child experience reading success and a love of reading for life!

Best wishes,

Charlotte Raby and Emily Guille-Marrett

Series editors of the Collins *Big Cat Phonics for Letters and Sounds* series

© HarperCollins*Publishers* 2018

Using Letters and Sounds

Big Cat Phonics for Letters and Sounds books match directly to Letters and Sounds. The phonemes and graphemes covered in each band are shown below.

Phase of Letters and Sounds	*Big Cat Phonics for Letters and Sounds* Book Band	New phonemes and graphemes	Review phonemes and graphemes
Phase 1	**Lilac** (I Spy)	• Aspect 1: General sound discrimination – environmental sounds • Aspect 2: General sound discrimination – instrumental sounds • Aspect 3: General sound discrimination – body percussion • Aspect 4: Rhythm and rhyme • Aspect 5: Alliteration • Aspect 6: Voice sounds • Aspect 7: Oral blending and segmenting	
Phase 2	**Pink A** (Chant and Chatter)	s, a, t, p, i, n, m, d	
	Pink B (Chant and Chatter)	f, h, b, g, o, c, k, e, u, r, l, ck (ff, ll, ss)	s, a, t, p, i, n, m, d
Phase 3	**Red A**	j, v, w, x, y, z, zz, qu, ch, sh, th, ng, nk	s, a, t, p, i, n, m, d, f, h, b, g, o, c, k, e, u, r, l, ck, ff, ll, ss
	Red B	ai, ee, igh, oa, *oo*, oo, ar, or, ur, ow, oi, ear, air, ure, er	s, a, t, p, i, n, m, d, f, h, b, g, o, c, k, e, u, r, l, ck, ff, ll, ss, j, v, w, x, y, z, zz, qu, ch, sh, th, ng, nk
Phase 4	**Yellow**	blend two or three adjacent consonants at the beginning, middle and end of words using only short vowel sounds: a, e, i, o, u	ai, ee, igh, oa, *oo*, oo, ar, or, ur, ow, oi, ear, air, ure, er
	Blue	blend two or three adjacent consonants at the beginning, middle and end of words with long vowel sounds: ai, ee, igh, oa, *oo*, oo, ar, or, ur, ow, oi, ear, air, ure, er	blend two or three adjacent consonants at the beginning, middle and end of words using only short vowel sounds: a, e, i, o, u

Teaching phonics

Until children become fluent at reading, they need daily systematic phonics practice. Every day, teach a new sound and review a few sounds children have been taught already. Make sure your phonics teaching has a lively pace. This part of the lesson should last 10 minutes at the most.

Example lesson plan: teaching the phoneme /ee/

Preparation

- Write the letters **ee** onto a card.
- Make some cards with words containing the new grapheme **ee**.
- Put sound buttons or dashes under each grapheme.
- Make some cards each with a different familiar grapheme.
- Make some cards with words made up of these familiar graphemes (some with sound buttons and dashes, and some without).
- Make some alien word cards made up of these familiar graphemes.

6   © HarperCollins*Publishers* 2018

Using Letters and Sounds

Oral practice
- Say the new sound **/ee/**. Tell children to repeat the sound.
- Sound out a word: **sh/ee/p**.
- Ask children to repeat the sounds and blend the word.
- Repeat with a few other words containing **ee**: **keep**, **seen**, **tree**.
- Make sure children understand what each word means, giving examples if needed.

Read the sounds
- Show children the card with **ee** written on it and say the sound: **/ee/**. Explain that the two letters make one sound.
- Show children one word card with **ee** at a time, asking them to read the word. Do not read the word for them!
- If children cannot read a word, model reading it.

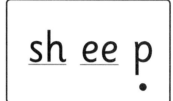

Review sounds and words
- Review the sounds children already know: show them the cards one at a time and correct any misconceptions.
- Show the word cards with familiar graphemes that have sound buttons and dashes. Encourage children to read the words by sounding out each grapheme in turn. Remind them that letters with a dash beneath them make one sound.
- Show the word cards with familiar graphemes without sound buttons or dashes. Ask children to read the word in their heads. Then ask them to read the word at speed without sounding out.

Alien words
- Show children the alien word cards with familiar graphemes. Ask them to look for any digraphs or trigraphs before they sound out and blend the word.

Spelling

Reading and spelling are reversible processes. Children blend to read and segment to spell. Ensure you teach spelling as part of your daily phonics sessions.

Teach children to segment words using new graphemes.

How to teach segmentation
- Say the word.
- Say the sounds in the word.
- Ask children to put up one finger for each sound.
- Tell children to say the word and then point to each finger as they say each sound.

Writing the word
- Show children how to say the word and then write the sounds in the word on a board.
- Wipe the word away.
- Ask children to say the word and then write the sounds.
- Show children the correct spelling and ask them to check (and correct) their spelling.

Practise speedier spelling with review graphemes. This time, encourage children to be more independent.
- Say the word.
- Ask children to repeat the word and work out the number of sounds.
- Ask children to say the word, counting the sounds with their fingers.

Writing the word
- Ask children to write the word.
- Show children the correct spelling and ask them to check (and correct) their spelling.

© HarperCollins*Publishers* 2018

Curriculum coverage

Coverage of the EYFS Early Learning Goals

Big Cat Phonics for Letters and Sounds books cover the Early Learning Goals for Communication and Language, Reading and Writing, and fully support the 2017 Statutory Framework for the Early Years Foundation Stage.

All *Big Cat Phonics for Letters and Sounds* books at Bands Lilac to Yellow cover the following Early Learning Goals:

ELG 01 Listening and attention
Children listen attentively in a range of situations. They listen to stories, accurately anticipating key events, and respond to what they hear with relevant comments, questions or actions. They give their attention to what others say and respond appropriately, while engaged in another activity.

ELG 02 Understanding
Children follow instructions involving several ideas or actions. They answer 'how' and 'why' questions about their experiences and in response to stories or events.

ELG 03 Speaking
Children express themselves effectively, showing awareness of listeners' needs. They use past, present and future forms accurately when talking about events that have happened or are to happen in the future. They develop their own narratives and explanations by connecting ideas or events.

ELG 08 Making relationships
Children play co-operatively, taking turns with others. They take account of one another's ideas about how to organise their activity. They show sensitivity to others' needs and feelings, and form positive relationships with adults and other children.

ELG 09 Reading
Children read and understand simple sentences. They use phonic knowledge to decode regular words and read them aloud accurately. They also read some common irregular words. They demonstrate understanding when talking with others about what they have read.

ELG 10 Writing
Children use their phonic knowledge to write words in ways which match their spoken sounds. They also write some irregular common words. They write simple sentences which can be read by themselves and others. Some words are spelt correctly and others are phonetically plausible.

ELG 17 Being imaginative
Children use what they have learnt about media and materials in original ways, thinking about uses and purposes. They represent their own ideas, thoughts and feelings through design and technology, art, music, dance, role play and stories.

All Lilac books also cover:

ELG 15 Technology
Children recognise that a range of technology is used in places such as homes and schools. They select and use technology for particular purposes.

Additional Early Learning Goals for each book can be found in the table opposite and explained in the list that follows.

© HarperCollins*Publishers* 2018

Additional Early Learning Goals

Book Band	Book Title	Early Learning Goals
Lilac	Number Fun	ELG 11 Numbers
	Animal Fun Sound Walk	ELG 14 The world
	My Day, Our World	ELG 14 The world ELG 13 People and communities
Pink A	Pat it Pit Pat Sip it Tip it	ELG 14 The world
Pink B	Dig it Up on Deck	ELG 14 The world
Red A	Big Mud Run	ELG 14 The world
	In the Fish Tank	ELG 06 Self-confidence and self-awareness
	This is My Kit	ELG 06 Self-confidence and self-awareness ELG 15 Technology
	Fantastic Yak Up in a Rocket	ELG 17 Being imaginative
Red B	Get Set For Fun It is Hidden	ELG 14 The world
	Look at Them Go	ELG 15 Technology
Yellow	How the Ear Can Hear	ELG 14 The world ELG 05 Health and self-care
	From the Top The Foolish, Timid Rabbit	ELG 14 The world
	Stunt Jets	ELG 12 Shape, space and measures ELG 16 Exploring and using media and materials ELG 04 Moving and handling
	In the Frog Bog	ELG 07 Managing feelings and behaviour
	The Best Vest Quest	ELG 16 Exploring and using media and materials

ELG 04 Moving and handling
Children show good control and coordination in large and small movements. They move confidently in a range of ways, safely negotiating space. They handle equipment and tools effectively, including pencils for writing.

ELG 05 Health and self-care
Children know the importance for good health of physical exercise, and a healthy diet, and talk about ways to keep healthy and safe. They manage their own basic hygiene and personal needs successfully, including dressing and going to the toilet independently.

ELG 06 Self-confidence and self-awareness
Children are confident to try new activities, and to say why they like some activities more than others.They are confident to speak in a familiar group, will talk about their ideas, and will choose the resources they need for their chosen activities. They say when they do or don't need help.

© HarperCollins*Publishers* 2018

Curriculum coverage

ELG 07 Managing feelings and behaviour
Children talk about how they and others show feelings, talk about their own and others' behaviour, and its consequences, and know that some behaviour is unacceptable. They work as part of a group or class, and understand and follow the rules. They adjust their behaviour to different situations, and take changes of routine in their stride.

ELG 11 Numbers
Children count reliably with numbers from 1 to 20, place them in order and say which number is one more or one less than a given number. Using quantities and objects, they add and subtract two single-digit numbers and count on or back to find the answer. They solve problems, including doubling, halving and sharing.

ELG 12 Shape, space and measures
Children use everyday language to talk about size, weight, capacity, position, distance, time and money to compare quantities and objects and to solve problems. They recognise, create and describe patterns. They explore characteristics of everyday objects and shapes and use mathematical language to describe them.

ELG 13 People and communities
Children talk about past and present events in their own lives and in the lives of family members. They know that other children don't always enjoy the same things, and are sensitive to this. They know about similarities and differences between themselves and others, and among families, communities and traditions.

ELG 14 The world
Children know about similarities and differences in relation to places, objects, materials and living things. They talk about the features of their own immediate environment and how environments might vary from one another. They make observations of animals and plants and explain why some things occur, and talk about changes.

ELG 16 Exploring and using media and materials
Children sing songs, make music and dance, and experiment with ways of changing them. They safely use and explore a variety of materials, tools and techniques, experimenting with colour, design, texture, form and function.

The Phonics Screening Check

Schools that teach children the graphemes from Phases 2 and 3 of Letters and Sounds during Reception are laying a firm foundation for success in the Phonics Screening Check in Year 1.

Most of Section 1 of the Phonics Screening Check is covered in Phases 2 and 3 (see table below).

Children who are confident in reading the graphemes in Phase 2 and the long vowel graphemes in Phase 3 will find blending adjacent consonants easy.

If children learn to read the long vowel graphemes in Reception they will find learning the alternate long vowel graphemes much easier.

Note: Graphemes should be taught *before* they are encountered in the books.

Section 1 of the Phonics Screening Check		
Grapheme-Phoneme Correspondence	***Big Cat Phonics for Letters and Sounds* Book Band**	**Phase in Letters and Sounds**
s, a, t, p, i, n, m, d	Pink A	2
f, h, b, g, o, c, k, e, u, r, l, ck, ff, ll, ss	Pink B	2
j, v, w, x, y, z qu, zz ch, ng, sh, th, nk	Red A	3
ar, ee, oi, oo, *oo*, or	Red B	3
Adjacent consonants	Yellow Blue	4

Section 2 of the Phonics Screening Check		
Grapheme-Phoneme Correspondence	***Big Cat Phonics for Letters and Sounds* Book Band**	**Phase in Letters and Sounds**
/z/ s ai, igh, air, ur, oa, er, ow	Red A Red B	3
Adjacent consonants	Yellow Blue	4

Steps for success in the Phonics Screening Check

- Regularly **review** graphemes from previous phases.
- Teach the alternate vowel graphemes in Phase 5 cumulatively. As soon as children are confident with the new vowel grapheme, review all the other ways to spell the same sound.
- Practise reading words with adjacent consonants. Make sure children can read words with adjacent consonants, and long and short vowel sounds.
- Practise reading two-syllable words with graphemes from Section 1, such as: lemon, rocket.
- Practise reading two-syllable words with graphemes from Section 2, such as: spoiler, lighter, turning.
- Practise reading 'alien' words with the graphemes children know well. Make sure children read each sound and then blend – do not encourage children to read these words without blending.
- **Never** teach children to spell 'alien' words.

© HarperCollins*Publishers* 2018

The *Big Cat Phonics for Letters and Sounds* view of reading

A reader does more than just read the words on the page, and that's why we have developed lesson plans and resources to ensure your children become fluent, engaged readers who understand and learn from the books they read.

- Children who find reading easy enjoy it.
- Children who can connect what they read to their own experiences and books that have been read to them see reading as a reflection of their world.
- These children grow their world and their imaginations through reading.
- They meet new words and expand their vocabulary.
- Reading helps them express themselves better and helps them become better writers: a virtuous positive cycle.

Use the lesson plans and resources alongside the *Collins Big Cat Phonics for Letters and Sounds* books (which are linked to Letters and Sounds) and unlock the wonderful world of reading for all your children.

All aspects of reading – phonics, vocabulary and comprehension – add up to reading for pleasure: fluency and fun.

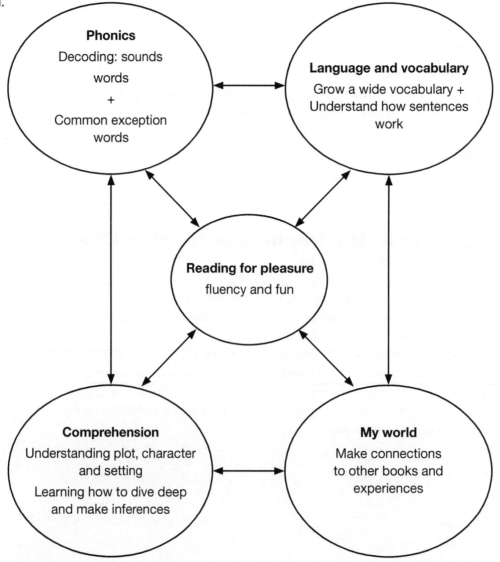

Reading skills

Decoding

- Assess children using the assessments on pages 26–34 to ensure they are reading books at the right band.
- Use the grouping grid on page 35 to find out which graphemes to teach children so they make speedy progress.
- Teach phonics daily using the short, fun activities. Reinforce children's phonic knowledge with the lesson plans, activity sheets and I Spy or Reader Response activities for every book.
- Use the example lesson plan on pages 6–7 to teach new graphemes, and review and reinforce previous learning.

Common exception words

- Use the example lesson plan on pages 22–23 to teach the common exception words before children read each book.
- Regularly review common exception words so children can read them fluently.
- See progression in the common exception words table on page 169.

Language and vocabulary

- Integrate teaching the meaning of words as children are learning to read.
- Read books to children with ambitious vocabulary. Explore the meaning of these words and challenge children to use them. Inspire a sense of wonder and curiosity about the world of words.
- Expand children's vocabulary with the lesson plans, resource sheets and activities for every book.
- Create a word wall to collect all the ambitious vocabulary children have read and heard.

My world

- Read to your class every day – the greater a child's store of stories, the more they will be able to connect to the stories they read. They will be able to imagine the world of the story more vividly, and so enjoy the books they read even more.
- Read non-fiction to children. Lemov and Willingham[1] both agree that reading about the world is as crucial as reading stories. Reading non-fiction expands children's knowledge of the world and increases vocabulary.
- Choose a wide variety of books and consider having a 'school canon': a list of books every child will have had read to them by the time they leave primary school.

Comprehension

- Bring each *Big Cat Phonics for Letters and Sounds* book alive by exploring the rich illustrations and photographs.
- Use vivid language to describe the action, setting and characters in the early books.
- Use the *Reading for pleasure* booklists to explore other books with similar themes.
- Ensure children have a basic understanding of the texts and can go deeper using the lesson plans and resource sheets in this handbook, in addition to the *Talk about it* section and comprehension activities on the inside cover of the *Big Cat Phonics for Letters and Sounds* books.

---

1 Doug Lemov *Reading Reconsidered* 2016
  Daniel Willingham *Why don't students like school?* 2009

Starting the reading journey with *Big Cat Phonics for Letters and Sounds*

Children begin Reception bringing a variety of skills and reading experiences to start their learning journey at school. Some children will have experienced singing nursery rhymes and being spoken with and read to regularly with parents/carers, and others may never have experienced sharing books or traditional nursery rhymes. Phase 1 of Letters and Sounds is critical for all children and offers every child the opportunity to build and secure a strong foundation for success for learning to read with phonics.

Foundation for phonics

Phase 1 should be taught throughout Reception and the Lilac books are perfect for children to read and re-read during this time. These books have been created to encourage children to talk, listen, expand their vocabulary and chant nursery rhymes. They encourage activities that link directly to the Phase 1 objectives. The Lilac fiction and non-fiction books have been written by the *Big Cat Phonics for Letters and Sounds* Series Editors, who are passionate about the importance of Phase 1 and its impact on phonics and reading success later on. Inspired by classic picture books and beautifully illustrated and photographed, the books also encourage children's natural curiosity to explore the images, with the aim of engaging them and nurturing reading for pleasure.

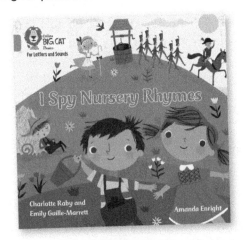

Children are ready to move on to the Pink *Chant and Chatter* books when they have successfully completed the Big Cat Phonics Assessment to check they are ready for this stage. Throughout the *Big Cat Phonics for Letters and Sounds* journey there are assessments to ensure children are secure in their phonics knowledge and are ready to move on to the next band. See pages 26–34 for more on Big Cat Phonics Assessment.

Phonics, fluency and fun!
At school

Children should be taught new sounds every day as a whole class and then read the books at the appropriate band in small groups. Sounds are introduced to match the order in Letters and Sounds and support your phonics teaching. Each book between Lilac and Red A ends with an *I Spy* phonics activity to practise and consolidate learning. From Red B through to Turquoise the final spread contains a *Reader Response* section, in line with other Big Cat books, which provides support for monitoring comprehension and promoting further discussion.

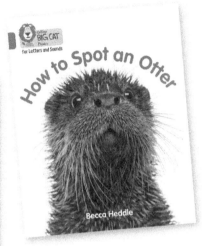

For independent reading, children need to be secure at 95% without any decoding in order to read with speed and fluency. This naturally supports their reading comprehension and develops confidence through success. A child who experiences success in reading is likely to enjoy reading and want to read. If you share a range of fiction and non-fiction books with children alongside the *Big Cat Phonics for Letters and Sounds* books, children will continue to experience reading for pleasure. We know that children who continue to read for pleasure are more likely to succeed academically, and there is evidence to suggest that reading supports emotional well-being and promotes tolerance of others.

At home

In addition to reading the *Big Cat Phonics for Letters and Sounds* books in groups in the classroom, children can enjoy the stories and non-fiction texts at home with parents. As well as linking to the Letters and Sounds phases, all the *Big Cat Phonics for Letters and Sounds* books are book banded to integrate easily into your classroom resources.

It is important to explain to parents that when children bring their *Big Cat Phonics for Letters and Sounds* books home they should be having fun. Fluency levels should be high, so children can 'show off' to their parents and practise other important reading skills, such as reading with expression.

Reading for pleasure

Throughout the lesson plans we have recommended a small selection of picture books that link to the book's subject, themes or relevant reading skills. Teachers can share these with children in class, or parents/carers may enjoy reading them to children at home. Children may choose a picture book they cannot yet decode but which is fun to engage with and explore, either making up their own version of the story as they turn the pages or experiencing the joy of being a reader by mimicking repetitive phrases they have heard read to them, such as *We're Going on a Bear Hunt* by Michael Rosen and Helen Oxenbury. Exploring pictures in books also encourages discussion, imagination and understanding.

© HarperCollins*Publishers* 2018

Becoming a reading school

Creating a reading school

Children need to know why reading is important – in the context of both reading for purpose and reading for pleasure. Positive experiences children have reading at home and at school will form a foundation for reading for life. How they see adults and children respond to books and reading material will form their view of reading too.

Reading for purpose

Reading for purpose encompasses all the things we need to read: environmental print such as menus, street signs, shopping lists, tickets and posters; formal and informal letters, bills and news; and information online. From the earliest years, children learn that marks have meaning in the world around us, such as logos and road signs.

Having examples of all these types of reading material in role-play areas and appropriate places around the school will encourage children to experience how reading can help us to function effectively – and will help them to see the value and purpose of printed materials.

Reading for pleasure

Studies have shown far-reaching benefits for children reading for pleasure, including: academic success at school; creative and imaginative thinking; relationship building; developing empathy; feeling self-confident; improving well-being. But how can you create an exciting and engaging reading experience for every child?

In this Teaching Handbook we have suggested a link to every Collins *Big Cat Phonics for Letters and Sounds* learning to read book. As children practise their phonics and common exception words, they will gain further reading experiences by being read to aloud. These include: the connection and enjoyment of sharing books together; the pleasure of reading widely; forming personal opinions on literature; understanding different author voices and illustration styles; deeper comprehension skills; how to read fluently and with expression; the experience of a rich and wide vocabulary – and more!

1. Read to your children every day

To help integrate reading stories into your busy day, have a selection of 'read aloud' books that are easy to access, link to cross-curricular topics and match the needs and interests of children in your class.

Ensure you have a range of books that can be integrated into the busiest of days. We often think of reading a story as quiet time, and this is an important practice, but some books can energise children and be read with the children standing up and wiggling around, which is a perfect choice just before break time. You might like to try this with *If You're Happy and You Know It* by Jan Ormerod and Lyndsey Gardiner.

Choose non-fiction books to go alongside the fiction you read to children. Lemov (*Reading Reconsidered* 2016) and Willingham (*Why don't students like school?* 2009) both agree that reading about the world is as crucial as reading stories. Reading non-fiction expands children's knowledge of our world and increases vocabulary.

When a child has a wordless book they drive its narrative, becoming both the reader and the story creator. This type of book also encourages book talk, helps build a rich vocabulary, develops comprehension skills and helps children experience positive book behaviours. If parents understand the merit in wordless books and are supported in understanding how to use them, they can be great for sending home. Children can curl up, there is no pressure to decode and they can have fun with their grown-up. Wordless books are accessible to everyone, regardless of language or literacy, and can help every family to enjoy books.

Further reading on this topic:
- Michael Morpurgo on reading to children every day – *The power of stories*, Michael Morpurgo's Book Trust lecture, Thursday 22nd September, michaelmorpurgo.com.
- Neil Gaiman on the importance of libraries – Neil Gaiman: Why our future depends on libraries, reading and daydreaming, *The Guardian*, 15th October 2013.

2. Be a children's reading expert

It is important that your classroom, and hopefully your school library, is full of a variety of engaging and inspiring children's books – fiction, non-fiction and reference. To do that effectively involves engaging with children's literature in a meaningful way and becoming an expert in it (if you're not already). Knowing books deeply can significantly strengthen your ability to support the needs, interests and preferences of each child, and help you to find ways to engage and encourage them to experience a wide range of books.

Becoming a children's reading expert isn't as hard as it sounds – there are so many ways to get information on children's books. Building strong relationships with local libraries is a great way to get advice and is a practical way of replenishing books in your classroom when budgets are tight. Social media can be used to follow the latest news, reviews and book awards, helping you to stay up to speed with new literary talent and trends popular with children. Some authors and illustrators you might like to follow are: Chris Riddell – you can watch him draw live; the Children's Laureate; and Michael Rosen, who writes a regular blog.

Being a reading expert goes beyond what we are familiar with. Take a look at your reading collection and consider how inclusive it is. When children see characters like themselves in picture books, it can help them relate to the story and it allows them to see their place in children's literature. And while it's important to ensure characters are represented in stories, it is also critical for every child that they experience authors, illustrators, poets and story makers from a range of cultures. Be committed to ensuring that your classroom includes a diverse range of stories, characters, authors and illustrators.

Some useful resources include:

- BookTrust bookfinder
- National Literacy Trust book lists
- Little Parachutes book finder
- Open University 'Teachers as Readers' research project
- Scottish Book Trust: 'Creating a Reading Culture: Get your whole school reading'
- Beanstalk on how to match books to a child
- Just Imagine podcast 'In the Reading Corner: Reading for Pleasure'

3. Sing nursery rhymes every day

Nursery rhymes are important to help children experience rhythm, rhyme and alliteration – all of which are important for learning to read with phonics. Many of these traditional rhymes are little stories in their own right, for example, they have a beginning, middle and end, characters, a setting and a plot. They also encourage children to experience enjoyment from a rich and unusual vocabulary. And, they encourage reading for meaning, and finding pleasure from words and pictures in a creative and imaginative way.

4. Organise visits from authors, illustrators, poets and storytellers

Children rarely have the opportunity to connect with story makers and performers any more. Making links with organisations such as Patron of Reading or the Society for Storytelling can help create a reading culture in your school that will inspire children to see value in reading, writing and storytelling. Remember, hearing authors read from their books, illustrators draw ideas and stories, and oral storytellers perform their work, shows stories and books are much more than the mechanics of reading and writing.

It isn't always practical to arrange author visits, but there is a huge variety of fantastic videos now available for children to watch, and you could even suggest live streaming Q&A sessions to your classroom with reading practitioners.

5. Positive reading models

Do your children see you and other teachers reading for pleasure? Talk to the children about what book you are reading and encourage parents and carers to do the same. What books have you recently taken out from the library or bought? Have you been to any book signings or literary events? Consider who is reading to the children, for example, evidence shows that boys respond well to seeing men read as well as women.

Try to ensure that discussions include what you're reading online as well as physical books: reading does not always appear as visibly as it did in the past – newspapers and books were piled high rather than stored digitally.

Reading volunteers who listen to children read bring such great value to schools, as we are all aware, but you can also encourage local people to come in and tell stories. This is a great way of engaging families from all backgrounds in exploring stories and rhymes from their own cultural heritage – regardless of English-speaking or literacy levels.

© HarperCollins*Publishers* 2018

Big Cat Phonics for Letters and Sounds chart

Book title	Book Band	Phase in Letters and Sounds	I Spy focus	Phonic focus	Common exception words	Fiction/ Non fiction
Number Fun	Lilac/Band 0	1		n/a	n/a	Fiction
I Spy Nursery Rhymes	Lilac/Band 0	1		n/a	n/a	Fiction
I Spy Fairytales	Lilac/Band 0	1		n/a	n/a	Fiction
Animal Fun	Lilac/Band 0	1		n/a	n/a	Non-fiction
Sound Walk	Lilac/Band 0	1		n/a	n/a	Non-fiction
My Day, Our World	Lilac/Band 0	1		n/a	n/a	Non-fiction
Pat it	Pink A/Band 1A	2	s	s, a, t, p, i, n	n/a	Fiction
Pit Pat	Pink A/Band 1A	2	a	s, a, t, p, i, n	n/a	Non-fiction
Sip it	Pink A/Band 1A	2	n, d	s, a, t, p, i, n, d	a	Non-fiction
Map Man	Pink A/Band 1A	2	p	s, a, t, p, i, n, m, d	n/a	Fiction
Pip Pip Pip	Pink A/Band 1A	2	i, m	s, a, t, p, i, n, m, d	a, is	Fiction
Tip it	Pink A/Band 1A	2	t	a, t, p, i, n, m, d	a	Non-fiction
Dig it	Pink B/Band 1B	2	g, o	g, o	a, is, the	Non-fiction
Not a Pot	Pink B/Band 1B	2	c, k, ck	g, o, c, k, ck	a, is, the	Fiction
Pop Pop Pop!	Pink B/Band 1B	2	e, u	g, o, ck, e, u	a, to, the, no, go	Fiction
Up on Deck	Pink B/Band 1B	2	r, h	o, ck, e, u, r, h	a, is, has, the, I	Non-fiction
Mog and Mim	Pink B/Band 1B	2	b, f, ff	g, o, ck, e, u, r, h, b, f, ff	is, to, the	Fiction
Bad Luck, Dad	Pink B/Band 1B	2	l, ll, ss	g, o, c, k, ck, e, u, r, h, b, f, ff, l, ll, ss	a, as, the, no, go, I	Non-fiction
This is My Kit	Red A/Band 2A	3	th, ng, ch	x, zz, ch, th, ng, nk	my, to, the, go, push	Non-fiction
Zip and Zigzag	Red A/Band 2A	3	j, v	j, v, z, qu, th, nk	to, the, go, we, they	Fiction
Big Mud Run	Red A/Band 2A	3	w, qu	j, w, z, qu, sh, th, ng, nk	to, the, go, are, they, you	Non-fiction
Fantastic Yak	Red A/Band 2A	3	x, y	x, y, ch, th, nk	I, her, was, you,	Fiction
In the Fish Tank	Red A/Band 2A	3	sh, nk	j, x, y, z, sh, nk	the, put, my	Non-fiction
Up in a Rocket	Red A/Band 2A	3	z, zz	w, z, zz, sh, ng	I, my, we, was	Fiction

© HarperCollins*Publishers* 2018

Big Cat Phonics for Letters and Sounds chart

Book title	Book Band	Phase in Letters and Sounds	I Spy focus	Phonic focus	Common exception words	Fiction/ Non fiction
Pink Boat, Pink Car	Red B/Band 2B	3		/ar/ /ow/ /oa/ /oo/ /oo/ /ure/ /ur/ /oi/ /air/ /ee/	the, I, are, my, we, they, your	Fiction
A Bee on a Lark	Red B/Band 2B	3		/ee/ /ar/ /oa/ /er/ /oo/ tt	the, they	Fiction
Wow Cow!	Red B/Band 2B	3		/oa/ /ee/ /oo/ /ar/ /ow/ /ear/ /oo/ /ur/ nn, pp	the, no, her, you	Fiction
Get Set For Fun	Red B/Band 2B	3		/oo/ /ar/ /ai/ /ow/ /oo/ /ear/ /ee/ /or/ /igh/ /er/ dd	the, go, by, put	Non-fiction
It is Hidden	Red B/Band 2B	3		/ee/ /oo/ /or/ /oa/ /ar/ /igh/ /oo/ /er/ /ow/, dd, tt	to, the, you, by	Non-fiction
Look at Them Go	Red B/Band 2B	3		/ar/ /oo/ /ow/ /ear/ /er/ /oo/ /ee/ /ur/ /ai/ /air/ /tt, bb	the, go, pull, push, they	Non-fiction
The Best Vest Quest	Yellow/Band 3	4		Read words with short vowel sounds with the adjacent consonants: st, spl, ft, sm, fr, nd, nt, sn, scr	of, to, the, I, all, my, be, was, little	Fiction
From the Top	Yellow/Band 3	4		Read words with short vowel sounds with the adjacent consonants: fr, nd, sp, gr, spr, st, bl, fl, cl	of, to, the, by, you, house	Non-fiction
In the Frog Bog	Yellow/Band 3	4		Read words with short vowel sounds with the adjacent consonants: st, spl, mp, pl, nd, fr, gr	to, the, go, all, are, we, you, they, like, so, little, ask	Fiction
Stunt Jets	Yellow/Band 3	4		Read words with short vowel sounds with the adjacent consonants: ft, nd, pr, st, nt, fl, sw, sp, tw, dr, gr	to, the, you	Non-fiction
The Foolish, Timid Rabbit	Yellow/Band 3	4		Read words with short vowel sounds with the adjacent consonants: cr, st, sp, sn, spl, nt, mp, pl, sk	to, the, I, by, he, we, was, you, they	Fiction
How the Ear Can Hear	Yellow/Band 3	4		Read words with short vowel sounds with the adjacent consonants: lp, mp, spl, scr, st, cr, dr, ct, lf	of, to, the, by, are, you, they, have, like, do, come, little, out, what	Non-fiction
Jump On, Jump Off!	Blue/Band 4	4		Read words with long vowel sounds with the adjacent consonants: st, sp, sl, br, gr, sc, tr, sw, fl, cl, cr	to, the, by, are, she, we, me, be, you, so, there, out, ask	Fiction
Eggs on Toast	Blue/Band 4	4		Read words with long vowel sounds with the adjacent consonants: st, pl, cr, sw, pr, sp, sc, gr, br, squ, thr	of, to, the, I, all, are, she, you, they, some, little, out, love	Fiction
Tusks	Blue/Band 4	4		Read words with long vowel sounds with the adjacent consonants: st, fr, gr, nt, sl, scr, sp	of, to, the, all, are, my, he, me, was, you, they, said, were, there, one, out, your, love, our	Fiction

© HarperCollins*Publishers* 2018

Big Cat Phonics for Letters and Sounds chart

Book title	Book Band	Phase in Letters and Sounds	I Spy focus	Phonic focus	Common exception words	Fiction/Non fiction
Athletics	Blue/Band 4	4		Read words with long vowel sounds with the adjacent consonants: tr, sp, fl, cl, st, cr	of, to, the, into, you, they, have, what	Non-fiction
How to Spot an Otter	Blue/Band 4	4		Read words with long vowel sounds with the adjacent consonants: sl, br, thr, cl, st, sm, sp, lt, fr, tw, cr, tr	of, to, by, the, are, be, you, they, like, do, little, when, out, what,	Non-fiction
Maps	Blue/Band 4	4		Read words with long vowel sounds with the adjacent consonants: nt, st, fl, cl, tr, sm, sp, str, gr, lt, pl	of, to, the, no, go (ago), all, are, we, be, was, you, they, have, so, were, there, one, what, our	Non-fiction
The Elf and the Bootmaker	Green/Band 5	5		/ai/ ay, ey, a-e, /igh/ i, i-e, /oa/ o, o-e, /oo/ ue, ew, ui, u-e, /ee/ ea, /oi/ oy, /ow/ ou, /el/ ea, /i/ y, /u/ o-e, /ar/ a, /or/ aw, al, /air/ ere, are, /ur/ ir, or, ear	of, to, the, into, my, he, she, we, said, were, one, what, once	Fiction
Monster Treat	Green/Band 5	5		/ai/ ay, ey, a-e, /u/ o-e, /igh/ i, i-e, /ur/ ir, /oo/ ui, u-e, ew, ue, /ow/ ou, /el/ ea, /ol/ a, /oo/ oul, /oa/ ow, /ee/ ea, /ar/ a	to, the, she, we, me, said, so, do, when, what, oh	Fiction
Where Did My Dingo Go?	Green/Band 5	5		/oa/ o, ow, /oo/ ue, u, /air/ ear, /ee/ ea, /ai/ a-e, ay, ey, /igh/ i-e, i, /i/ y, /oo/ oul, /or/ al	oh, friend, where, of, into, the, my, she, me, said, have, so, one	Fiction
Bear Spotting	Green/Band 5	5		/ai/ ay, ei, ey, a-e, /igh/ i, i-e, /oa/ o, ow, ol, o-e, /oo/ u, ou, /ee/ ea, /ow/ ou, /ar/ a, /or/ augh, aw, al, /ure/ our, /air/ ear, are, ere, /ur/ ir, or, /ear/ eer, /el/, ea, /u/ o	of, to, the, into, by, are, we, be, have, so, one, where, house, their	Non-fiction
How Not to be Eaten	Green/Band 5	5		/ee/ ea, ie, /e/ ea, /ai/ ay, a-e, /igh/ i-e, /oo/ u-e, ew, ou, /oa/ o, o-e, /or/ al, our /o/ a, /ow/ ou, /u/ o-e, /ar/ a, /air/ are /oo/ oul, /ur/ ir	of, to, the, into, put, are, be, have, so	Non-fiction
How to Draw Cat and Dog	Green/Band 5	5		/ar/ a, /or/ aw, our, al, /ow/ ou, /ai/ a-e, /e/ ea, /igh/ i-e, i, /ee/ ea, /ure/ our, /oa/ o, ow, o-e	where, of, to, the, put	Non-fiction
Watch Out, Nebit!	Orange/Band 6	5		/f/ ph, /w/ wh, /ee/ e-e, y, /igh/ y, /ch/ tch, /j/ g, ge, dge, /l/ le, /z/ se, /sh/ ch, /ai/ a	of, to, the, into, are, one, oh, their, friend	Fiction
Disaster Duck	Orange/Band 6	5		/w/ wh, /f/ ph, /igh/ ie, y, /ee/ y, e-e, e, /j/ g, ge, /ch/ tch, /c/ ch, /l/ le, /sh/ ch	of, to, the, one, were, oh	Fiction
Noisy Neesha	Orange/Band 6	5		/ee/ e, ey, y, /l/ le, /oo/ u, /igh/ y, /ai/ a, /z/ se, /v/ ve, /f/ ph, /w/ wh	of, to, the, are, said, Mr, Mrs, friend, were	Fiction
Beetles Around the World	Orange/Band 6	5		/igh/ y, ie, /ee/ y, e, /w/ wh, /v/ ve, /l/ le, /ch/ t, /ai/ a, /j/ g, ge, /f/ ph, /z/ se	of, to, the, into, are, were, their, people	Non-fiction

Big Cat Phonics for Letters and Sounds chart

Book title	Book Band	Phase in Letters and Sounds	I Spy focus	Phonic focus	Common exception words	Fiction/ Non fiction
The Equator	Orange/Band 6	5		/ai/ a, eigh, /ee/ y, e-e, e, ey, /igh/ y, /j/ ge, g, /l/ le, /f/ ph, /z/ se, /ch/ tch, t, /w/ wh, /v/ ve, /c/ ch, t, /s/ se	of, to, the, into, their, people	Non-fiction
Smart Gadgets	Orange/Band 6	5		/ai/ a, /ee/ e-e, y, e, /igh/ y, /w/ wh, /sh/ ch, /c/ ch, /j/ g, ge, /f/ ph, /z/ se, /ch/ t, /l/ le	of, to, the, into, do, one, were, their, people, today	Non-fiction
Jake and Jen in the Tomb of Ice	Turquoise/Band 7	5–6		/sh/ ti, ssi, /m/ mb, /n/ kn, gn, /r/ wr, zh /s/ ce, sc, /zh/ sur	of, to, the, into, are, said, were, one, their, water	Fiction
Nibble, Nosh and Gnasher	Turquoise/Band 7	5–6		/r/ wr, /s/ c, /n/ gn, kn, /c/ que, x, /sh/ ci, /m/ mb	of, to, the, into, said, so, were, one, friend, great	Fiction
Living Fossils	Turquoise/Band 7	5–6		/m/ mb, /s/ sc c, /sh/ si ci	of, to, the, into, are, so, do, were, their, today, water, many, shoe	Non-fiction
Space Science	Turquoise/Band 7	5–6		/n/ kn, /s/ sc, ce, c, /sh/ ssi, ti, /zh/ s	of, to, the, into, are, so, were, one, our, their, people, because, break, many, who, half	Non-fiction
Big Questions	Turquoise/Band 7	5–6		/n/ kn, /r/ wr, /s/ sc c ce, /sh/ ti si ci	of, to, the, into, are, so, do, one, our, their, because, water, many, move, eye	Non-fiction
The Dragon King's Daughter	Turquoise/Band 7	5–6		/n/ kn, gn /m/ mb, /s/ c, ce /zh/ su, /sh/ ti, si, ssi	of, to, the, into, are, said, so, were, because, water, any, many	Fiction

© HarperCollins*Publishers* 2018

Teaching common exception words with *Big Cat Phonics for Letters and Sounds*

When to teach common exception words

In order to ensure complete coverage of Letters and Sounds and National Curriculum expectations we have combined the Common Exception Word lists for Year 1 and Year 2 with the Tricky Words linked to each phase of Letters and Sounds.

Common exception words in *Big Cat Phonics for Letters and Sounds*

Year	*Big Cat Phonics for Letters and Sounds* Book Band	Phase in Letters and Sounds	National Curriculum	Letters and Sounds
Reception	**Pink A** (Chant and Chatter)	2	a, is	
	Pink B (Chant and Chatter)	2	a, as, is, of, his, has	to, the, no, go, I, into
	Red A and **B**	3	put, pull, full, push	he, she, we, me, be, was, you, they, all, my, her
Year 1	**Yellow**	4	house, here, once, ask	said, have, like, so, do, some, come, were, there, little, one, when, out, what
	Blue	4	school, your, love, our	

Please refer to the chart on page 169 to find out when common exception words become decodable.

How to teach common exception words

Common exception words are commonly-used words that contain an unusual grapheme. This makes them difficult to read using phonics alone. We need to teach children which part of the word is the 'tricky bit', and alert them to how this grapheme is said. Follow the example lesson plan below to help children read common exception words. Make sure you do this before they meet the words in the books.

Regular practice of common exception words will help to move these words into children's orthographic store, and then they will be able to read the words fluently.

Example lesson plan: teaching the common exception word 'they'

- Write (or print) the word **they** onto card.
- Show children the word on the card.
- Say the word **they**.
- Ask children to repeat the word.
- Tell children that **they** has two graphemes: th/ey. Draw a line under each grapheme to show that they are digraphs:

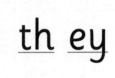

- Read each grapheme in turn. Explain that the second grapheme is the 'tricky bit'. Circle the tricky grapheme in red.
- Read the word together.
- Ask children to read the word to you.

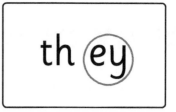

Reviewing common exception words

Use the marked-up word cards from previous sessions.

Also write (or print) a 'clean' version of each word onto card (without sound buttons or dashes).

Use the marked-up words initially, moving on to the 'clean' versions as children become more confident.

- Tell children you are going to see how well they can read tricky words.
- Show children a word.
- Ask them to think about the tricky bit.
- Ask them to sound out each grapheme in order and read the word.
- If children can do this, ask them to read the word 'at speed' without sounding out.
- If they have problems with the 'tricky bit', go back and teach them the unusual grapheme.
- If children are confident, use the 'clean' version of the word to see if they can read the tricky word at speed.

Fluency in reading

When we teach children to read, we use books closely matched to their phonic knowledge so they can practise what they know and in this way become confident readers. We want every child to gain a sense of reading fluently every time they read a *Big Cat Phonics for Letters and Sounds* book.

Learning to read requires enormous effort, and we know that when children's cognitive load is over-burdened they are less successful (see recent research below). Children who practise reading books with the graphemes they already know are more successful and have a more positive attitude to reading. This is why it is vital that you choose books for your children at an instructional level that is at least **90% word accuracy** (D. C Parker and M K Burns, 2014). This means children should be able to read most of the text without hesitation and only need to work out, on average, one word in ten. Please use the assessments on pages 26–34 to place children at the correct stage.

What is reading fluency?

Reading fluency is not just reading quickly.[2] Fluency combines accuracy, automaticity and reading with expression. Children reading at 90 words per minute or more are able to concentrate on these other aspects of reading and can begin to think about what they are reading as they read. Reading fluency is a vehicle for reading comprehension.

Reading fluency needs to be taught from the very beginning, so every child feels that they have fully understood each book and that they can read each book with feeling. Each time a child reads like an expert reader they are laying down the skills that will help them fully engage with and enjoy the books they read independently later on.

Learning to read with fluency

1. Prepare for reading
   - Read the graphemes covered in the book.
   - Read the phonically regular words.
   - Read the common exception words.
   - Make connections to the book.
2. First reading
   - Read a page at a time, taking time to enjoy the pictures.
3. Second reading
   - The adult reads some or all of the book to children, modelling intonation, expression and emotion when reading dialogue.
   - Choose a double page for children to prepare reading with expression.
   - Discuss what words mean and how to read smoothly and with appropriate expression.
   - Try out voices for characters if there is dialogue!
4. Third reading
   - Read the book a final time.
   - Ask children to think about what is happening as they read.
   - Ask children to use expression on the pages they practised.

Curriculum objectives for the end of Year 1:
   - to read aloud books closely matched to their improving phonic knowledge, sounding out unfamiliar words accurately, automatically and without undue hesitation
   - to re-read these books to build up their fluency and confidence in word reading
   - to check that the text makes sense to them as they read and correcting inaccurate reading.

With practice children become fluent readers, but this takes time. By the time children are reading Turquoise band books they should be developing a fluent reading style. You should notice children reading smoothly and working out new words quickly without needing to overtly sound them out.

---

2 Cotter, Jennifer. 'Understanding the Relationship between Reading Fluency and Reading Comprehension: Fluency Strategies as a focus for Instruction' *Education Masters* Paper 224, 2012.

Big Cat Phonics assessment

Use the Big Cat Phonics assessments to work out which band of book each child should be reading.

Instructional reading level is at 90% word accuracy. This is the correct level of challenge for children when they are being taught to read and when they are practising the phonemes and graphemes they already know.

Note:
Reading at home: Independent reading level should be at 95% word accuracy, so that children are successful when they are reading without an adult's support.

Of course, this doesn't mean that parents and carers cannot read and share a wide range of picture books with their child at home. Indeed, this is essential for developing a love of literature and learning a wide range of skills, such as developing a rich vocabulary.

Teacher instructions: termly assessments

- Use these assessments every six weeks to check children's progress.
- Start the assessment at the level the child was secure at the last time they were assessed. Do not go back to the beginning.
- Use the grouping grid on page 35 to work out which book band is appropriate for each child.
- The grouping grid also has guidance on which graphemes to teach at each band of Big Cat Phonics.

Tick each grapheme or word that is read correctly.
Circle any word or part of a word that is read incorrectly.

Say the sounds. Ask the child to repeat the sounds and blend the word. It is acceptable if a child automatically blends the word without sounding out.

Ask the child to read each sound in order and blend them to read. It is acceptable if a child automatically blends the word without sounding out.

Tell the child that these are nonsense or alien words. They will not make sense! Ask the child to read each sound in order and blend them to read.

Ask the child to read the words without blending. Tell them to say the sounds in their head before reading. If they cannot read the word without blending, draw a wavy line above the word.

Term 1 teacher assessment sheet

Student name: _____ Class: _____ Date: _____

Book Band: Pink A/Band 1A	
New graphemes	s a t p i n m d
Oral	p-i-n m-a-t s-i-p

Book Band: Pink B/Band 1B	
New graphemes	f h b g o c k e u r l ck ff ll ss
Read and blend	hot cup peck gas

Book Band: Red A/Band 2A	
New graphemes	j v w x y z zz qu sh ch th ng nk
Sound out and blend	zip vet jam quick shut with chip
Alien words	fozz juck beng

Book Band: Red B/Band 2B	
New graphemes	ai ee igh oa *oo* oo ar or er
Sound out and blend	main see high goat book for shark zoom quicker hammer market
Alien words	joap laif charb

Book Band: Yellow/Band 3	
Review graphemes	ur ow oi ear air ure er
Sound out and blend	turn fear crack cow chair spring join sure list
Read without sounding (HFW)	this then down look
Alien words	scresh prib crat

Book Band: Blue/Band 4	
Sound out and blend	bright green spoilt spear boast train frighten groom
Read without sounding (HFW)	went from just help
Alien words	spaim plear cloig

© HarperCollins*Publishers* 2018

Term 1 student assessment sheet – part 1

Student name: _____ Class: _____ Date: _____

| Pink A/Band 1A | a | s a t p i n m d |

| Pink B/Band 1B | a | s a t p i n m d |
| | b | hot   cup   peck   gas |

Red A/Band 2A	a	j v w x y z zz qu sh ch th ng nk
	b	zip vet jam quick shut with chip
		fozz juck beng

Red B/Band 2B	a	ai ee igh oa *oo* oo ar or er
	b	main see high goat book for shark zoom quicker hammer market
		joap laif charb

© HarperCollins*Publishers* 2018

Term 1 student assessment sheet – part 2

Student name: _____ Class: _____ Date: _____

Yellow/Band 3

a	ur ow oi ear air ure er
b	turn fear crack cow chair spring join sure list
	this then down look
	scresh prib crat

Blue/Band 4

b	bright green spoilt spear boast train frighten groom
	went from just help
	spaim plear cloig

28 © HarperCollins*Publishers* 2018

Term 2 teacher assessment sheet

Student name: _____ Class: _____ Date: _____

Book Band: Pink A/Band 1A

New graphemes	p d t s n i m a
Oral	t-i-p s-a-t d-i-p

Book Band: Pink B/Band 1B

New graphemes	o e b g f c k h u l r ff ck ss ll
Read and blend	peg sun off big

Book Band: Red A/Band 2A

New graphemes	x z w j y v ng ch th qu sh zz nk
Sound out and blend	yet job fox buzz much thank wish
Alien words	quig zong kesh

Book Band: Red B/Band 2B

New graphemes	or oo igh er *oo* ee ar ai oa
Sound out and blend	meet sigh room look chain coat horn car rocker thicker pocket
Alien words	yeep thoot jorb

Book Band: Yellow/Band 3

Review graphemes	ow ur er ure air ear oi
Sound out and blend	hear town lunch boil pure stamp fair surf scrap
Read without sounding (HFW)	that them now too
Alien words	cromp hest flub

Book Band: Blue/Band 4

Sound out and blend	lair clown sprain screech point slight starlight gloom
Read without sounding (HFW)	help just from went

© HarperCollins*Publishers* 2018

Term 2 student assessment sheet – part 1

Student name: _____   Class: _____   Date: _____

Pink A/ Band 1A	a	p d t s n i m a
Pink B/Band 1B	a	o e b g f c k h u l r ff ck ss ll
	b	peg sun off big
Red A/Band 2A	a	x z w j y v ng ch th qu sh zz nk
	b	yet job fox buzz much thank wish
		quig zong kesh
Red B/Band 2B	a	or oo igh er oo ee ar ai oa
	b	meet sigh room look chain coat horn car rocker thicker pocket
		yeep thoot jorb

© HarperCollins*Publishers* 2018

Term 2 student assessment sheet – part 2

Student name: _____ Class: _____ Date: _____

Yellow/Band 3

a ow ur er ure air ear oi

b hear town lunch boil pure
stamp fair surf scrap

that them now too

cromp hest flub

Blue/Band 4

b lair clown sprain screech
point slight starlight gloom

help just from went

woint bloog trowp

© HarperCollins*Publishers* 2018

31

Term 3 Teacher assessment sheet

Student name: _____ Class: _____ Date: _____

Book Band: Pink A/Band 1A	
New graphemes	m d n i t s p a
Oral	m-a-p t-a-p s-i-t

Book Band: Pink B/Band 1B	
New graphemes	g e r o f k c h l u b ck ff ll ss
Read and blend	not dug miss get

Book Band: Red A/Band 2A	
New graphemes	z x j w v y ch ng qu th nk zz sh
Sound out and blend	box yap jet quack fish thing chop
Alien words	vezz wush chss

Book Band: Red B/Band 2B	
New graphemes	oo or er igh ee oo ai ar oa
Sound out and blend	week moon corn tight took rain coach hard chicken shorter better
Alien words	bighp gork feesh

Book Band: Yellow/Band 3	
Review graphemes	ur ow ure er ear air oi
Sound out and blend	hurt sure splat year pair bump owl coin trip
Read without sounding (HFW)	with yes for see
Alien words	brip lont stax

Book Band: Blue/Band 4	
Sound out and blend	creep spoon toast brown flight joint treetop strain
Read without sounding (HFW)	from just went help
Alien words	spreem grair dright

© HarperCollins*Publishers* 2018

Term 3 student assessment sheet – part 1

Student name: _____ Class: _____ Date: _____

Pink A/Band 1A	a	m d n i t s p a

Pink B/Band 1B	a	g e r o f k c h l u b ck ff ll ss
	b	not dug miss get

Red A/Band 2A	a	z x j w v y ch ng qu th nk zz sh
	b	box yap jet quack fish thing chop
		vezz wush chss

Red B/Band 2B	a	oo or er igh ee oo ai ar oa
	b	week moon corn tight took rain coach hard chicken shorter better
		bighp gork feesh

© HarperCollins*Publishers* 2018

Term 3 student assessment sheet – part 2

Name: _____

Yellow/Band 3	a	ur ow ure er ear air oi
	b	hurt sure splat year pair bump owl coin trip
		with yes for see
		brip lont stax

Blue/Band 4	b	creep spoon toast brown flight joint treetop strain
		from just went help
		spreem grair dright

34

© HarperCollins*Publishers* 2018

Big Cat Phonics assessment

Grouping grid

Book Band	Children are ready to read the books at this band when they can:	Teach these sounds to prepare for the next band:
Pink A/ Band 1A	Read without hesitation: s a t p i n m d Oral practice: repeat the sounds back and blend the words	f, h, b, g, o, c, k, e, u, r, l, ck ff, ll, ss
Pink B/ Band 1B	Read without hesitation: f h b g o c k e u r l ck ff ll ss Sound out and blend at least three words.	j, v, w, x, y, z zz, qu sh, ch, th, ng, nk
Red A/ Band 2A	Read without hesitation: j v w x y z zz qu sh ch th ng nk Sound out and blend at least five words. Sound out and blend at least two alien words.	ai, ee, igh, oa, *oo*, oo, ar, or, er
Red B/ Band 2B	Read without hesitation: ai ee igh oa *oo* oo ar or er Sound out and blend at least nine words. Sound out and blend at least two alien words.	Review: ur, ow, oi, ear, air, ure, er Teach: adjacent consonants with short vowel sounds
Yellow/ Band 3	Read without hesitation: ur ow oi ear air ure er Sound out and blend at least seven words. Reading without blending three high frequency words. Sound out and blend at least two alien words.	Review: ai, ee, igh, oa, *oo*, oo, ar, or, er, ur, ow, oi, ear, air, ure, er Teach: adjacent consonants with long vowel sounds
Blue/ Band 4	Sound out and blend at least six words. Reading without blending three high frequency words. Sound out and blend at least two alien words.	All alternate vowel graphemes (see Scope and Sequence: Green)

© HarperCollins*Publishers* 2018

Support for Lilac books
Introduction

> **Language development**
> - A large vocabulary is crucial to reading success.
> - Children need a vocabulary of 15,000 to 20,000 words to read children's literature successfully.
> - New vocabulary needs to be taught.
> - Children need to hear and use new words multiple times to fully understand them.
>
> Isabel L. Beck, Margaret G. McKeown and Linda Kucan, *Bringing Words to Life*, 2013

Nursery rhymes and language development

All the books in Lilac have nursery rhymes to support them (see page 174 onwards for our nursery rhyme collection). We suggest ideas of how to use them to best effect in the classroom and there is a resource sheet with a nursery rhyme focus to accompany the phonics and comprehension for each *Big Cat Phonics for Letters and Sounds* title.

> **Links to Phase 1 of Letters and Sounds**
>
> The six Collins *Big Cat Phonics for Letters and Sounds* wordless books support Phase 1 Letters and Sounds. Phase 1 is relevant to children throughout their time in Reception. Children need a solid foundation in nursery rhymes, fairy tales and traditional tales to fully enjoy many children's books. The Phase 1 activities will help children develop an awareness of sounds around them, how words work through exploring rhythm, rhyme and alliteration as well as oral practice of blending and segmenting the sounds in words.
>
> Children do not need to complete Phase 1 activities to move on to learning the Phase 2 phonemes.

The table below shows the aspects of Phase 1 covered across the six books in the Lilac band.

Big Cat Phonics for Letters and Sounds book title	Aspects of Letters and Sounds Phase 1						
	Aspect 1: Environmental sounds	Aspect 2: Instrumental sounds	Aspect 3: Body percussion	Aspect 4: Rhythm and rhyme	Aspect 5: Alliteration	Aspect 6: Voice sounds	Aspect 7: Oral blending and segmenting
Number Fun	✓			✓		✓	✓
I Spy Nursery Rhymes		✓			✓		✓
I Spy Fairytales			✓	✓			✓
Animal Fun	✓	✓			✓		✓
Sound Walk	✓		✓			✓	✓
My Day, Our World		✓	✓	✓			✓

Reading for pleasure
- The worlds of fairy tales and nursery rhymes are explored in many children's books.
- Ensuring children have a good understanding of these genres will enable them to enjoy many more books. These enduring characters and themes crop up again and again throughout children's literature, even in books for older children, such as Harry Potter.
- We have recommended a list of books that will enhance children's enjoyment of all the Collins *Big Cat Phonics for Letters and Sounds* wordless books.

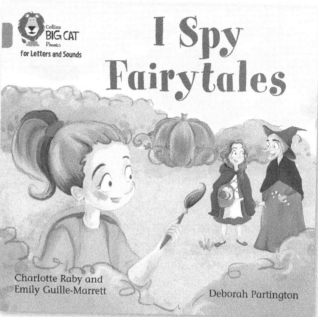
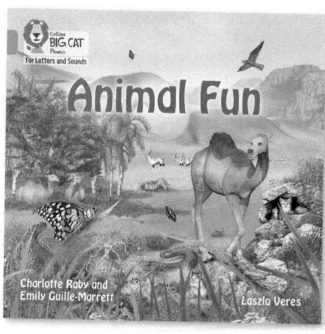

Preparing for Pink books (Chant and Chatter)
- Once children have settled into the routine in Reception, start teaching Phase 2 graphemes.
- Teach a sound a day. (See pages 6–7 for an example lesson plan.)
- Start teaching word reading as soon as children can read s, a, t, p, i and n without hesitation. (See page 68 for the steps in word reading.)
- Assess all Reception children once they have been taught all the Phase 2 phonemes. Use the assessment on pages 26–34 to place children at the appropriate book band.
- Use subsequent assessments every six weeks to ensure speedy progress.

Number Fun

Book band: Lilac

This book explores number nursery rhymes. Each picture relates to a number and a rhyme.

Practising phonics Phase 1

Warm up: Simon says

- Play 'Simon says' with farm animals. Sound out actions for children to do, for example: *Simon says p/e/ck like a hen, h/o/p like a rabbit* and so on.

Connect to prior knowledge

- Ask children if they know any number rhymes. Sing some of them together. Can children remember the actions?
- Use props to introduce the number rhymes and bring them to life. For example, use a toy mouse for *Hickory Dickory Dock* or ten teddies for *Ten in the Bed*.

Children read

- Let children enjoy reading the book by looking at the pictures.
- Explain to children how to spy the images next to the magnifying glass icon. Encourage children to spy and count the objects.
- Do children recognise any of the nursery rhymes or nursery rhyme characters in the book?

After reading

Sound discrimination: environmental sounds

- Ask children to suggest sounds they might hear in each picture. For example, in the first picture they might imagine hearing the clock ticking, the sounds of cooking in the kitchen, the cat purring or sounds coming in through the window from the garden.
- Encourage children to describe the sounds they imagine, using both words and sounds, such as a whooshing sound to imitate water.

Voice sounds

- Draw children's attention to how mother duck says 'quack, quack, quack, quack'. Ask children to think about the real sound ducks make. Can they imitate a duck? Encourage children to make a duck-like sound rather than saying the word **quack**.
- Can they make the sounds for the other animals in the book? Help children make sounds that approximate the animal noises. Can they change the tone and pitch of the sounds they make?

Oral blending and segmenting

- Play 'I spy sounds':
  - Show children one of the pictures from the book.
  - Use pure sounds to sound out something in the picture, for example: *I can see a c/a/t*.
  - Ask children to tell their partner what you can see.
  - Say the word in sounds: *c/a/t*, asking children to call out the word together.
  - Repeat for other words.

Rhythm and rhyme

- Clap the beat as you sing or say the number rhymes. Get children to join in with you to say the rhymes at the same speed.
- Help children hear the rhythm of the words.
  - Get children to copy you as you say and clap each syllable of multi-syllable words such as **hick/or/y**.
  - Start slowly and speed up as children become more confident.
  - Encourage children to clap the syllables in their names.
- Play 'I spy a rhyme'. Emphasise the final word of a line and ask children to clap when they hear its rhyming partner. Extend this game by slowing down as you get to the end of the line with the rhyming word in it. Can children jump in and predict the rhyming word?
- Challenge: Rhyme makers
  - Choose a number rhyme with a regular rhyming pattern like *Five Little Ducks*.
  - Help children identify the pairs of rhyming words (**day/away**, **quack/back**).
  - Work together to come up with other words that also rhyme with these words (for example, **stay/play/hey/neigh**, **stack/hack/rack/Jack**).
  - Say the rhyme again, this time getting children to choose different rhyming words to make a silly version.

Extending vocabulary

- Ensure children understand the meaning of the rhyming words.
- Model using the words in context.
- Praise children when they use these new words.

Comprehension

- Ask children to say the nursery rhyme *Hickory Dickory Dock* with you. Talk about the characters and plot in the rhyme. Ask: *When did the mouse come back down?*

- Use **Number Fun: Resource sheet 3** to sequence the events of the nursery rhyme with children. Ask children to do this independently.
- Repeat for the other nursery rhyme, *Five Little Ducks*.

Reading for pleasure

Whoosh Around the Mulberry Bush Jan Ormerod and Lindsey Gardiner

My Granny Went to Market: A Round-the-world Counting Rhyme Stella Blackstone and Christopher Corr

Ten Little Pirates Mike Brownlow and Simon Rickerty

Nursery Rhymes Lucy Cousins

Each Peach Pear Plum Janet and Allan Ahlberg

Nursery rhymes

Hickory Dickory Dock

Pussy Cat, Pussy Cat

Two Little Dickie Birds

Five Little Ducks

One, Two, Three, Four, Five

Ten in the Bed

Round and Round the Garden

Number Fun: Resource sheet 1
Phonics

Name: _____

What sounds do these animals make?

Match the pictures that rhyme.

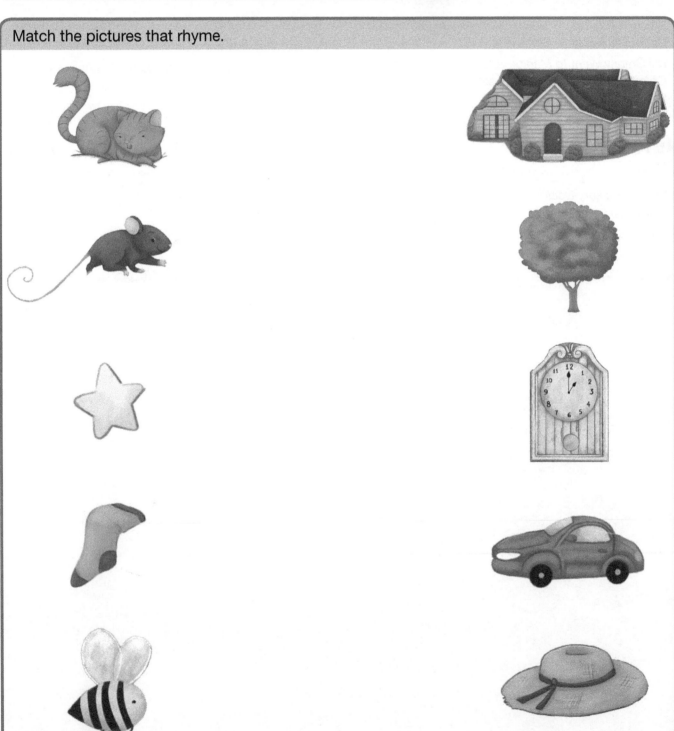

40 Lilac: Number Fun

Number Fun: Resource sheet 2
Comprehension

Name: _____

Match each character to the correct object.

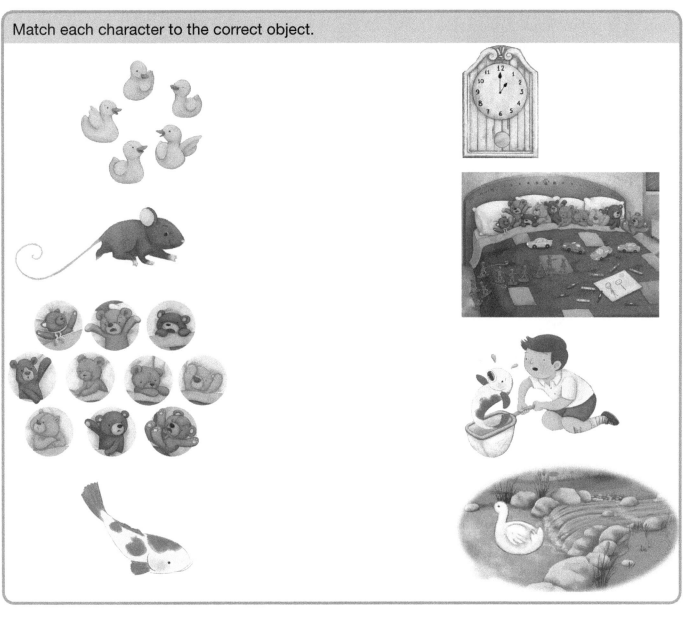

How many things can you count?

© HarperCollinsPublishers 2018   Lilac: Number Fun

Number Fun: Resource sheet 3
Nursery rhyme

Name: _____

Say or sing the nursery rhyme *Five Little Ducks*. See page 2 of the Nursery Rhymes booklet for the words. Can you put the nursery rhyme in the correct order?

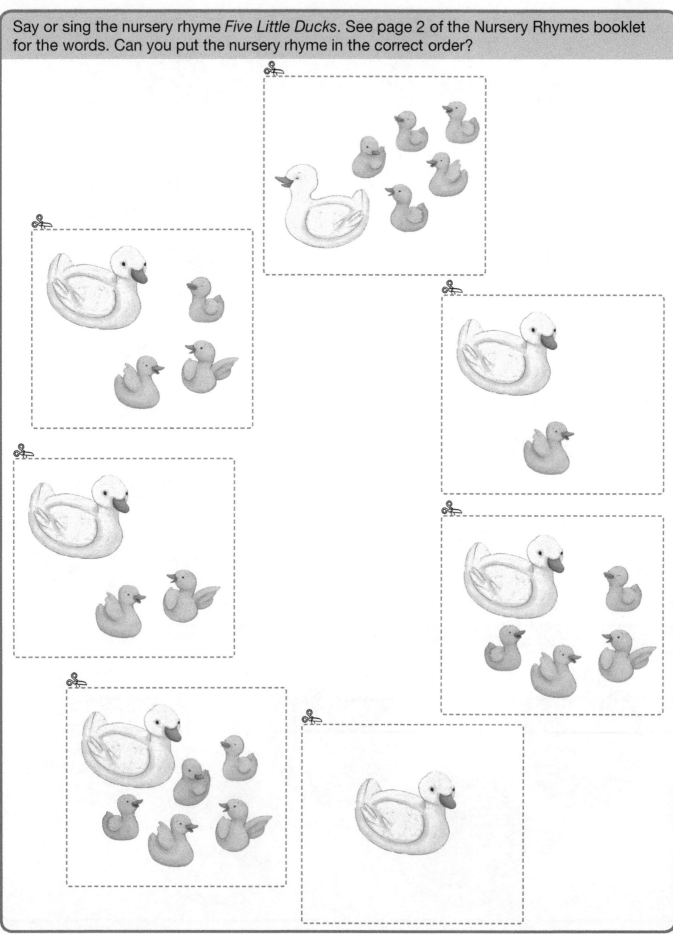

I Spy Nursery Rhymes

Book band: Lilac

In this book, we follow Jack and Jill as they travel through Nursery Rhyme Land.

Practising phonics Phase 1

Warm up: I spy
- Play 'I spy' with objects from the nursery rhymes: *I spy with my little eye something with the sounds f/i/sh.*
- Can children repeat the sounds and blend them to say the word?
- Repeat for other objects in the book: **bun**, **hill**, **duck**, **shell**, **cat**, **house** and **shoe**.

Connect to prior knowledge
- Ask children which nursery rhymes they know – sing some together with actions. Which are the children's favourites?
- Use props to introduce the nursery rhymes and bring them to life. For example, toy soldiers to march up the hill for *The Grand Old Duke of York* or buns on a tray for *Five Currant Buns*.
- Make the role play area into a nursery rhyme setting such as the village. Include writing opportunities as well as props to bring the nursery rhyme world to life.

Children read
- Let children enjoy reading the book by looking at the pictures.
- Explain to children how to spy the images next to the magnifying glass icon. Encourage children to spy and find the objects.
- Do children recognise any of the nursery rhymes, characters or locations in the book?

After reading

Alliteration
- Tell children that some of the nursery rhyme characters have names that start with the same sound, for example: Baa Baa black sheep. Ask children to listen as you say **Baa Baa black sheep** and ask: *Which sound is repeated in this character's name?* Say the name together emphasising the **/b/** sound.
- Repeat with the names: Muffin Man, Jack and Jill, crooked cat, Wee Willie Winkie and Little Boy Blue.
- Use **I Spy Nursery Rhymes: Resource sheet 1** to explore nursery rhyme characters that have alliterative names.
- Tell children they are going to help you make up a character with a name that starts with the same sounds. The character is a fish. Give children examples of words that do and do not alliterate: *Could it be: Johnny fish, Freddy fish, funny fish, lucky fish …?*

Sound discrimination: instrumental sounds
- Tell children they are going to march up and down the hill with the grand old Duke of York. Use a drum or tambourine to create a beat.
- Show children how to march or stomp in time.
- Vary the speed of the beat and see if children can recognise the change and adapt their pace.
- Give children instruments to beat. Ask them to copy the beat you are making.
- Give children the chance to lead the beat.

Oral blending and segmenting
- Play 'Which one?':
  - Lay out a range of objects from the story, for example: wool, horn, horse, bells, cake, bird, star and so on.
  - Check children know what each of the objects is, and relate them back to the story.
  - Say the sounds of an object for example: *s/t/ar*.
  - Ask children to repeat the sounds and blend them.
  - Can they say the word and point to the object?
  - Repeat for the other objects.

Extending vocabulary
- Nursery rhymes contain lots of prepositional/adverbial language.
- Help children learn the meaning of words such as: **over**, **under**, **up**, **down**, **behind**, **to**, **with**, **upon**, **on**, **in**, **top**, **after** and so on, by acting them out in the nursery rhymes.
- Change the prepositions/adverbs in a nursery rhyme and see how it changes what happens. For example: *Jack and Jill went over the hill to fetch a pail of water. Jack fell behind and broke his crown and Jill came tumbling to the bottom.*

Comprehension
- Look at all the characters Jack and Jill see. Can children work out who all the characters are?

© HarperCollins*Publishers* 2018

- Draw children's attention to objects associated with certain characters, for example, Mary and her little lamb, Little Boy Blue and his horn, the Baker and his buns and so on.

- Use **I Spy Nursery Rhymes: Resource sheet 2** to explore the objects associated with each character. Encourage children to look at the book to find their answers.

Reading for pleasure

Over the Hills and Far Away: A Treasury of Nursery Rhymes from Around the World Elizabeth Hammill

The Great Nursery Rhyme Disaster David Conway and Melanie Williamson

Quentin Blake's Nursery Rhyme Book Quentin Blake

Each Peach Pear Plum Janet and Allan Ahlberg

Tales from Acorn Wood Julia Donaldson and Axel Scheffler

Anno's Counting Book Mitsumasa Anno

The Very Hungry Caterpillar Eric Carle

One Gorilla: A Counting Book Anthony Browne

Have You Seen My Dragon? Steve Light

Tip Tap Went the Crab Tim Hopgood

Nursery rhymes

The Grand Old Duke of York

Jack and Jill

Little Bo Peep

Little Boy Blue

Baa Baa Black Sheep

Five Speckled Frogs

Five Little Ducks

Rub-a-Dub-Dub

Ride a Cock Horse

One, Two, Three, Four, Five

Row Row Row Your Boat

Horsey Horsey

Mary Mary Quite Contrary

There Was a Crooked Man

There Was an Old Woman Who Lived in a Shoe

Old MacDonald Had a Farm

Sing a Song of Sixpence

Five Currant Buns

Hot Cross Buns

Pat-a-Cake

Mary Had a Little Lamb

Wee Willie Winkie

Hey Diddle Diddle

Incy Wincy Spider

Rock-a-bye Baby

Hush Little Baby – Mockingbird

I Spy Nursery Rhymes: Resource sheet 1
Phonics

Name: _____

What sounds do these things make?

Say the names of these nursery rhyme characters. Can you hear the same letter sound repeated in their names?

Muffin Man

Wee Willie Winkie

Jack and Jill

Little Boy Blue

© HarperCollins*Publishers* 2018   Lilac: I Spy Nursery Rhymes

I Spy Nursery Rhymes: Resource sheet 2
Comprehension

Name: _____

Match each character to the right object.

How do Jack and Jill feel in the pictures?

I Spy Nursery Rhymes: Resource sheet 3
Nursery rhymes

Name: _____

Say or sing the nursery rhyme *Jack and Jill*. See page 6 of the Nursery Rhymes booklet for the words. Can you put the nursery rhyme in the correct order?

© HarperCollins*Publishers* 2018   Lilac: I Spy Nursery Rhymes   47

I Spy Fairytales

Book band: Lilac

This book follows a child as she travels along a path picking up lost objects belonging to fairytale characters.

Practising phonics Phase 1

Warm up: Point to the …
- Ask children to point to each object in the room after you sound it out. For example: *Point to the d/oor; point to the f/l/oor; point to the b/oo/k* and so on.
- After they have pointed, ask children to repeat the sounds and blend the word.

Connect to prior knowledge
- Ask children what they know about fairy tales or traditional tales.
- Talk about the different types of character in the stories: baddies like the Big Bad Wolf and the witch in Hansel and Gretel, and goodies like Little Red Riding Hood, Hansel and Gretel, and Jack.
- Ask children if they think Goldilocks is a goodie or a baddie. How would they describe her?

Children read
- Let children enjoy reading the book by looking at the pictures.
- Explain how to spy the images next to the magnifying glass icon. Encourage children to look at the objects the girl puts into her backpack.
- Do children recognise any of the fairy tales or characters in the book?

After reading

Rhythm and rhyme
- Tell children that words that rhyme have the same sound at the end. Start by saying some simple rhymes, for example, **cat**, **bat**, **sat** and **mat**. Ask children to repeat the rhyming words. Check they understand that the **at** at the end is making the rhyme.
- Play 'Odd one out'. Say three words, for example, **dog**, **leg** and **frog**. Ask children to shout the odd word out. Then ask them to say the rhyming words together.
- Look at the book and choose some of the objects or characters to make rhymes. For example: **cloak** and **croak**, **three bears** and **stairs**, **Jack** and **back** and so on.
- Play 'Rhyming bingo' using **I Spy Fairytales: Resource sheet 1**. Ask children to tick the picture when they hear you saying a word that rhymes with it. Words to use: **bear, cat, frog, mouse, tree, chair, hat, log, house, key**.

Sound discrimination: body percussion
- Tell children that you are the 'Pied Piper' and they must follow the music you make.
- Give children a movement, for example, skipping. Vary the tempo and see if children can match this as they skip.
- Ask children to make small movements when you play quietly and large movements when you play loudly.
- Ask children to decide which movement to do next.
- Talk about the types of sound you made and the movements children made.

Oral blending and segmenting
- Play 'I spy sounds':
  – Show children one of the pictures from the book.
  – Sound out something you can see in the picture, for example: *I can see a b/ear.*
  – Ask children to tell their partner what it is you can see.
  – Sound out again: *b/ear*. Ask children to call out the word together.
  – Ask children to find the bear in the book.
  – Repeat for other words.

Extending vocabulary
- Look at the objects the girl picks up as she walks through the forest (pages 12–13). Play 'Guess what?':
  – Choose one item and describe it to children without naming it. For example: *This is made of glass. It belongs to Cinderella and fits on her foot.*
  – Ask children to point to the object on the page when you have finished your description (and not before).
  – Repeat for the other objects.

Comprehension
- Look at the book together and talk about how the little girl is feeling on each page. Discuss how surprised she might feel when she sees the door into the fairytale world. Show children a look of surprise. Can they show you a surprised face?
- Use **I Spy Fairytales: Resource sheet 2** to talk about how each character from the story is feeling.

Reading for pleasure

Mixed Up Fairy Tales Hilary Robinson and Nick Sharratt

Prince Cinders Babette Cole

Princess Smartypants Babette Cole

Jack and the Baked Beanstalk Colin Stimpson

Very Little Red Riding Hood Teresa Heapy and Sue Heap

The Jolly Postman or Other People's Letters Janet and Allan Ahlberg

The Three Little Wolves and the Big Bad Pig Eugene Trivizas and Helen Oxenbury

The Magic Paintbrush

Little Red Riding Hood

Hansel and Gretel

Cinderella

Goldilocks and the Three Bears

Jack and the Beanstalk

Nursery rhymes

Pussy Cat, Pussy Cat

Teddy Bear, Teddy Bear

Five Speckled Frogs

Old MacDonald Had a Farm

Three Blind Mice

I Spy Fairytales: Resource sheet 1
Phonics

Name: _____

What noises might these things make?

Say the words and match the pictures that rhyme.

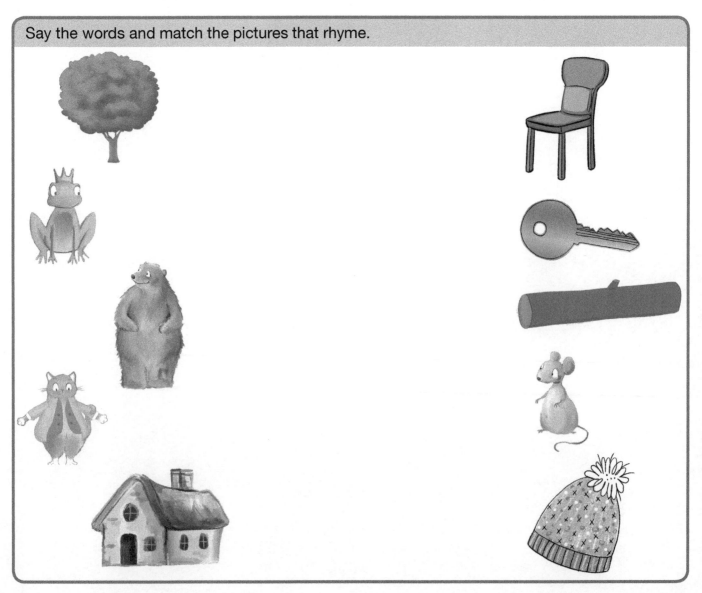

50   Lilac: I Spy Fairytales   © HarperCollins*Publishers* 2018

I Spy Fairytales: Resource sheet 2
Comprehension

Name: _____

Match each character to the right object.

How are the characters feeling?

© HarperCollins*Publishers* 2018　　　　　　　　　　　Lilac: I Spy Fairytales　　51

I Spy Fairytales: Resource sheet 3
Nursery rhymes

Name: _____

Say or sing the nursery rhyme *Teddy Bear, Teddy Bear*. Colour the teddy bear in.

52 Lilac: I Spy Fairytales © HarperCollins*Publishers* 2018

Animal Fun

Book band: Lilac

This book explores a range of habitats around the world and the animals that live there.

Practising phonics Phase 1

Warm up: Silly sandwiches
- Tell children you are going to make some silly sandwiches with crazy ingredients, but you can't say the word, you can only say the sounds.
- Introduce each ingredient by saying: *Silly sandwich on my plate, / What kind of sandwich shall I make? / I need a l/ea/f.*
- Ask children to help you by repeating the sounds and blending them into a word. When they say the correct word, add the ingredient to your sandwich.
- Repeat with other silly ingredients until you have made a very silly sandwich!

Connect to prior knowledge
- Ask children what they know about wild animals.
- Help them categorise animals into, for example, insects, birds, fish, mammals, amphibians and reptiles.
- Talk about habitats where children might expect to find a frog, a lion or a parrot.
- Ask children to think about their favourite animal. Do they know where it comes from?

Children read
- Let children enjoy reading the book by looking at the pictures.
- Explain to children how to spy the images next to the magnifying glass icon. Encourage children to look at different animals and details of each habitat.
- Do children recognise any of the habitats or animals in the book?

After reading

Sound discrimination: environmental sounds
- Look at the animals in the book and talk about the sounds they make. Some of the animals may be unfamiliar so children can guess or make up a sound for them.
- Encourage children to use their voices to make the sounds rather than saying the sound's name, for example, **woof** rather than **bark**.
- Play 'Sound lotto'. Give each child an animal lotto card (**Animal Fun: Resource sheet 1**). Make the sounds of the animals. Children tick the picture when they hear the animal's sound.

Alliteration
- Talk about how the animals move. Ask children to slink like a snake or leap like a leopard.
- Ask children if they can hear the first sounds of these two words: **slinking snake**. Take feedback.
- Repeat with: **leaping leopard**.
- Write a list of animals children have found in the book and work together to create alliterative actions for them.
- Get children to act out each alliterative animal action.

Sound discrimination: instrumental sounds
- Play 'Grandmother's footsteps'.
  - Tell children to line up side by side. Position yourself some distance away – you are 'Grandmother'.
  - Ask children to move like an animal as you bang on a drum. For example: *Hop like a bird; Slither like a snake; Creep like a hunting lion.*
  - Ask children to move towards you as you bang the drum, and freeze when the banging stops.
  - Face away from children while you bang the drum. When you stop banging the drum, quickly turn around to see if you can see anyone moving. If you catch any children, send them back to the starting line.

Extending vocabulary
- Discuss what the animals in the book look like. Some animals are brightly coloured so they stand out. Others are the same colour as their habitat so they blend in.
- Look through the book to find animals that blend in and stand out.
- Talk about how animals might benefit from blending in or standing out.
- Help children to compose sentences about specific animals that blend in or stand out: *The lion is a dull yellow colour so it blends in and can hunt its prey. The parrot has bright feathers so it stands out and can be seen by other parrots.*

© HarperCollins*Publishers* 2018

Comprehension

- Talk about the different habitats in the book.
- Ask children to point out the animals in each habitat. Can they name the animals?
- Discuss how the animals are well adapted to their environment, for example: *The monkeys have long, strong arms so they can climb easily and grasp at fruits. The ants work together to forage on the forest floor.*
- Encourage children to talk about the animals that interest them.
- Use **Animal Fun: Resource sheet 2** to match each animal to its habitat.

Reading for pleasure

Dear Zoo Rod Campbell

Brown Bear, Brown Bear, What Do You See? Bill Martin, Jr and Eric Carle

Abigail Catherine Rayner

Animal Ark: Celebrating Our Wild World in Poetry and Pictures Kwame Alexander and Joel Sartore

The Rainforest Grew All Around Susan K. Mitchell

What the Ladybird Heard Julia Donaldson and Lydia Monks

Flip Flap Jungle Axel Scheffler

Hug Jez Alborough

Can You Say it Too? Moo Moo! Sebastien Braun

Blown Away Rob Biddulph

From Head to Toe Eric Carle

Dogs Emily Gravett

Nursery rhymes

Old MacDonald Had a Farm

Five Little Ducks

Higgledy Piggledy My Black Hen

Down in the Jungle Where Nobody Goes

I Went to the Animal Fair

Five Little Monkeys Swinging in a Tree

An Elephant Goes Like This and That

Animal Fun: Resource sheet 1
Phonics

Name: _____

What sounds do these animals make?

Say the words and match the pictures that rhyme.

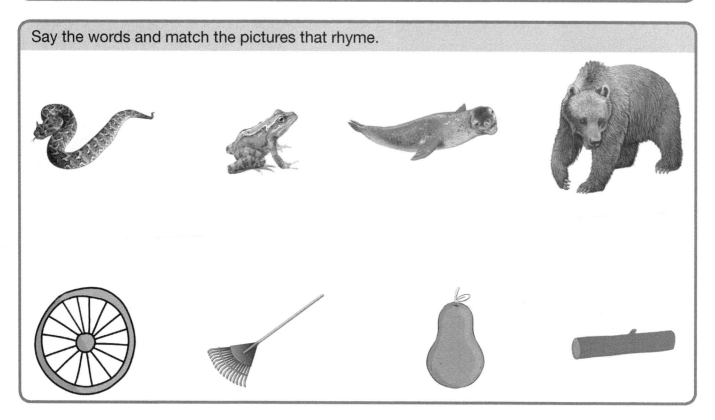

© HarperCollins*Publishers* 2018   Lilac: Animal Fun   55

Animal Fun: Resource sheet 2
Comprehension

Name: _____

Read the book. Match each animal to its habitat.

56   Lilac: Animal Fun   © HarperCollins*Publishers* 2018

Animal Fun: Resource sheet 3
Nursery rhymes

Name: _____

Say or sing the nursery rhyme *Old MacDonald Had a Farm*. See page 8 of the Nursery Rhymes booklet for the words. Use the animals in the pictures.
What noises do the animals make?

Sound Walk

Book band: Lilac

This book takes you on a sound walk, from home, through town, to the park and then the beach, where you can hear a carnival parade.

Practising phonics Phase 1

Warm up: I spy

- Play 'I spy' with objects from the book: *I spy with my little eye something with the sounds: b/u/s.*
- Can children repeat the sounds and blend them to say the word? (Use objects in the book: book, toy, rug, clock, car, pram, slide, bird, ball and drum.)

Connect to prior knowledge

- Ask children to talk about their walk to school. What do they see? What sounds do they hear? Take feedback.
- Ask children to think about the sounds they hear around their home. Which are loud sounds and which are quiet sounds? Take feedback.

- Ask children to talk about instruments they know. What sounds do they make? Take feedback.
- Ask children what they expect to hear on a sound walk. Take feedback.

Children read

- Let children enjoy reading the book by looking at the pictures.
- Explain to children how to spy the images next to the magnifying glass icon.
- Do children recognise any of the objects making sounds?
- Choose one of the locations in the book for your role-play area. Encourage children to make the sounds of the objects as they play.

After reading

Sound discrimination: environmental sounds

- Go on a sound walk with children. Start in the school, walking very quietly through the corridors, listening to sounds coming from classrooms. Stop by the office to hear the telephone, printer and talking. Stop at intervals to note the sounds children have heard as they walk.
- On your return make a sound map of the school. Which places are quiet and which are noisy?
- If possible, take children on a sound walk outside school. Get children to listen very carefully to the natural and human-made sounds around them. Can they locate where the sounds are coming from?

Sound discrimination: body percussion

- Sing action songs linked to the book:
  - *The Wheels on the Bus*: Encourage children to add new characters and new actions, for example: *The big kids on the bus all nod to songs …*
  - *Down by the Station*: Encourage children to make actions for the trains and other vehicles such as buses, motorboats, aeroplanes and so on.
  - *Polly Put the Kettle On*: Encourage children to join in with the actions.

Voice sounds

- Tell children they are going to create sound effects for one of the pages in the book.
- Choose a page and ask children to find the objects on that page that make sounds. Discuss the types of sounds each thing makes. Are the sounds low and humming or high and soft? Do the sounds drone on or do they come in short bursts? Do the sounds get louder as they go on?
- Ask children to experiment with sounds they make with their mouth. Can they use their tongue to make a clicking sound or take their voice down a slide?
- Once you have practised the sounds, work together to make the sounds for the different objects and bring the picture to life!

Extending vocabulary

- Make sounds for children to listen to using your voice, objects or instruments. If you are using instruments or objects, make the sound behind a screen so children cannot see what is making the sound. Help children describe the sounds using accurate vocabulary. Challenge children to say if a sound is: loud, quiet, high, low, long, short, clicking, buzzing, humming and so on.
- Ask children to make sounds for each other to describe.

Comprehension

- Ask children: *Which place in the book would you most like to go to? Why?* Take feedback.

58

© HarperCollins*Publishers* 2018

- Talk about which location might be the quietest or the noisiest. Discuss what children could do in each location.

- Ask questions to explore different aspects of each picture, such as: *Where would you have to be careful about traffic? Where could you go paddling? Where could you dance to music? Where could you relax?*

Reading for pleasure

At the Beach Roland Harvey

Busy, Busy World Richard Scarry

Out and About: A First Book of Poems Shirley Hughes

Charlie and Lola: We Honestly Can Look After Your Dog Lauren Child

Handa's Surprise Eileen Browne

Busy, Busy Town Richard Scarry

Shark in the Park! Nick Sharratt

Lucy & Tom At the Seaside Shirley Hughes

Can You Hear the Sea? Judy Cumberbatch and Ken Wilson-Max

Tanka Tanka Skunk! Steve Webb

All Join In Quentin Blake

And the Train goes... William Bee

Noisy Poems Jill Bennett and Nick Sharratt

Nursery rhymes

Pat-a-Cake

The Wheels on the Bus

Down by the Station (repeat for all vehicles)

Girls and Boys Come Out to Play

Hark Hark the Dogs do Bark

A Sailor Went to Sea

I Am the Music Man

Old King Cole

Polly Put the Kettle On

Sound Walk: Resource sheet 1
Phonics

Name: _____

What sounds do these things make?

1.

2.

3.

4.

Say the words.
Circle the picture that does NOT start with the same letter sound.

1.

2.

3.

Sound Walk: Resource sheet 2
Comprehension

Name: _____

Look at the pictures from the book. What might happen next?

© HarperCollins*Publishers* 2018　　　　　　　　　　Lilac: Sound Walk　　61

Sound Walk: Resource sheet 3
Nursery rhymes

Name: _____

Say or sing the song *The Wheels on the Bus*. Use the pictures to say the sounds.

My Day, Our World

Book band: Lilac

This book explores what children from all around the world do every day.

Practising phonics Phase 1

Warm up: Silly sandwiches
- Tell children you are going to make some silly sandwiches for lunch with crazy ingredients. You won't say the word, you will only say the sounds.
- Introduce each ingredient by saying: *Silly sandwich on my plate, / What kind of sandwich shall I make? / I need a d/o/ll.*
- Ask children to help you by repeating the sounds and blending them into a word. When they say the correct word, add the ingredient to your sandwich.
- Repeat with other silly ingredients until you have made a very silly sandwich!

Connect to prior knowledge
- Ask children about their routine. What do they do every day?
- Talk about the foods they eat for breakfast and supper, and discuss favourite foods.
- Discuss games children like to play at break times and at home. Which are their favourites?
- Talk about routines that keep you healthy, like brushing your teeth and sleeping.
- Discuss how every child does many of the same things as they do, no matter where they live.

Children read
- Let children enjoy reading the book by looking at the pictures.
- Explain to children how to spy the images next to the magnifying glass icon. Encourage them to look at details in the pictures and spot what is the same and what is different.
- Do children recognise any games that the children in the book play at school?

After reading

Sound discrimination: body percussion
- Talk about games children like to play at break time. Tell children that clapping and skipping games are popular around the world.
- Teach children how to clap with a partner to *Pat-a-Cake* (see Nursery Rhymes booklet, page 9). Use a simple clapping pattern.
- Play jumping games using a low skipping rope for children to jump over in a rhythm as they chant a simple rhyme such as: *I like coffee, I like tea. I like _____ to jump with me.*

Rhythm and rhyme
- Ask children to help you find some objects in the book you can make rhymes for. (Make sure they are one-syllable words.)
- Show children how you use the same final sound to make two words rhyme, for example: **bed** and **said**. Ask children to say another word that makes the same rhyme.
- Once children are confident, add a word that does not rhyme, for example: **book**, **late**, **hook**. Ask children to say which word is the odd one out.
- Ask children to look at the pictures on **My Day, Our World: Resource sheet 1** to work out which words rhyme.

Sound discrimination: instrumental sounds
- Talk about the activities children do every day to get ready for school. Make a list together, for example: brush my teeth, comb my hair, wash my face and so on.
- Teach children the song *This is the way I ...* using the actions from their list.
- As you sing, encourage some children to use instruments to keep the beat of the song and other children to do the actions. Swap over.

Extending vocabulary
- Help children use sequential language to order the events in the book, for example: **first**, **next**, **after that**, **then**, **finally**.
- Direct children to do simple activities using sequential language such as making a tower with bricks: *First collect six bricks. Then put a brick on the floor. After that put the bricks on top of each other until you have built a tower.*
- Encourage children to say their own sequences of instructions for a friend to carry out.

Comprehension
- Look at the pictures in the book in order and talk about the sequence of events in a day.
- Encourage children to talk about their day. Can they find the activities they do in the book?

© HarperCollins*Publishers* 2018

- Ask children to sequence the pictures showing a child's day on **My Day, Our World: Resource sheet 2**.

Reading for pleasure

Five Minutes' Peace Jill Murphy

Just Imagine Nick Sharratt and Pippa Goodhart

Can't You Sleep, Little Bear? Martin Waddell and Barbara Firth

Oh, The Places You'll Go! Dr. Seuss

My World, Your World Melanie Walsh

Nursery rhymes

Hickory Dickory Dock

Twinkle Twinkle

The Sun Has Got His Hat On

Here We Go Round the Mulberry Bush

Rock-a-bye Baby

Frère Jacques (Are You Sleeping?)

If You're Happy and You Know It

My Day, Our World: Resource sheet 1
Phonics

Name: _____

What sounds can you hear?

Say the words. Match the words that rhyme.

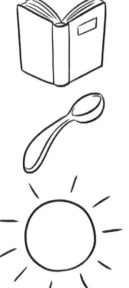

© HarperCollins*Publishers* 2018   Lilac: My Day, Our World   65

My Day, Our World: Resource sheet 2
Comprehension

Name: _____

What do you do in a day? Can you put these pictures in the right order?

66   Lilac: My Day, Our World   © HarperCollins*Publishers* 2018

My Day, Our World: Resource sheet 3
Nursery rhyme

Name: _____

Say or sing the nursery rhyme *Hickory Dickory Dock*. See page 6 of the Nursery Rhymes booklet. Use these pictures to help you.

Draw a picture of your favourite part of *Hickory Dickory Dock*.

Support for Pink books
Introduction

Cognitive load
- The working memory has finite capacity.
- Children need to practise new things until they are automatic before they move on.
- If new skills are layered on top of newly acquired learning it overloads the working memory.
- However, if new learning is practised it can be built on in small steps.
- Review is vital in moving new learning into the long-term memory.

Make sure children are reading books at the right band so that they are not overloading their working memory. Practising reading should be at 90% fluency, so the cognitive load is not too high.

Books 1–6

Teaching children to read words with the sounds they know:
- Teach a new sound every day: see page 70 'How to teach a new sound'.
- Review all known sounds until children are fluent.
- Once children know the sounds: **/s/**, **/a/**, **/t/**, **/p/**, **/i/**, **/n/**, teach them to read words using the steps below.

Steps in word reading
Step 1
- Say the word you are going to read: *tin.*
- Say the sounds as you put a card out for each letter: *t/i/n.*
- Sweep your finger beneath the letters from left to right as you blend to say the word **tin**.
- Ask children to repeat the process. Praise them for 'reading' the word.

> Only make words with letters that children are fluent at reading.
>
> Make the sessions quick and fun.
>
> Add in new letters to make new words as soon as children can read them.

As children gain confidence:

Step 2
- Do not model reading the word.
- Display the letters one at a time. Hesitate as you display each letter so children can jump in and read it.
- Sweep your finger beneath the letters from left to right, blending the word with children.
- Say the word clearly after children have read it so they can hear a perfect pronunciation.
- When children read the word without your help they are ready to read the words off cards.

> If children find reading a word tricky, go back to Step 1 or Step 2.
>
> Always make words with letters children are fluent at reading.

68   © HarperCollins*Publishers* 2018

Support for Pink books Introduction

Link to Phase 2

Sounds

Note: The books should be read in order.

Books 1 and 2:	/s/ /a/ /t/ /p/ /i/ /n/
Books 3 to 6:	/s/ /a/ /t/ /p/ /i/ /n/ /m/ /d/
Book 7:	/s/ /a/ /t/ /p/ /i/ /n/ /m/ /d/ /g/ /o/
Book 8:	/s/ /a/ /t/ /p/ /i/ /n/ /m/ /d/ /g/ /o/ /c/ /k/ /ck/
Book 9:	/s/ /a/ /t/ /p/ /i/ /n/ /m/ /d/ /g/ /o/ /c/ /k/ /ck/ /e/ /u/
Book 10:	/s/ /a/ /t/ /p/ /i/ /n/ /m/ /d/ /g/ /o/ /c/ /k/ /ck/ /e/ /u/ /r/ /h/
Book 11:	/s/ /a/ /t/ /p/ /i/ /n/ /m/ /d/ /g/ /o/ /c/ /k/ /ck/ /e/ /u/ /r/ /h/ /b/ /f/ ff
Book 12:	/s/ /a/ /t/ /p/ /i/ /n/ /m/ /d/ /g/ /o/ /c/ /k/ /ck/ /e/ /u/ /r/ /h/ /b/ /f/ ff /l/ ll, ss

High frequency words

it, in, at, dad, on, dog, can, not, get, up, mum, am, on, off, back, as, him

Common exception words

There aren't any common exception words in the first six books except the word **a**. You will read these common exception words in this order:

a, the, go, to, no, I, is, and

(See pages 22–23 'How to teach common exception words' for an example lesson plan.)

© HarperCollins*Publishers* 2018

69

How to teach a new sound

Every day, teach one new sound, and review all the sounds children have met already.

Use pure sounds without a **/schwa/** sound at the end.

> - These are the sounds you can elongate without making a **/schwa/** sound: **/s/ /n/ /m/ /f/ /sh/ /l/ /r/ /v/ /z/**
> - These sounds must be kept short. Repeat them when you teach them to children: **/a/ /b/ /c/ /k/ /d/ /e/ /g/ /h/ /i/ /j/ /o/ /p/ /qu/ /t/ /u/ /w/ /x/ /y/ /ch/ /ng/ /nk/**

Example lesson plan: teaching the new sound /a/

Hear and say the sound

- Tell children that they are learning a new sound **/a/**.
- Say **/a/** with pure sounds. Tell children to repeat the sound.

Assess: Watch children as they say the sound. Check they are making the right sound.

- Say some words that start with the focus sound **/a/**: **apple**, **ant**, **avocado**, **amber**, and so on.
- Say the names of any children whose names start with the focus sound **/a/**.

> **Tip:** Sometimes names and words start with the focus letter but not with the correct phoneme.
> **/a/** ambulance
> **/ai/** apricot
> The letter **a** makes the long vowel sound **/ai/** in apricot.

See and say the sound

- Use an image to represent the focus grapheme; for example, an apple for **a**.
- Say the sound **/a/ /a/ /a/** as you trace around the **a** shape of the apple. Say *apple* as you get to the bottom of the letter.
- Tell children to join in with you. Repeat a few times.
- Show children the grapheme **a** written on a card. Say the sound. Ask children to repeat the sound.
- Hide the card and ask children to say the sound each time they see it. Show the card with the grapheme multiple times until children are confident.
- Now tell children to say **/a/** when they see the grapheme and **apple** when they see the picture.

Say and write the sound

- Draw an apple in the shape of the grapheme **a** on the board. Say the letter formation as you write the letter: *Round the apple, up to the top and down to the bottom.*
- Ask children to do the same: drawing the 'apple' in the air with their dominant hand.
- Write the grapheme **a** next to the image of the apple. Say the sound **/a/** as you write the letter.
- Ask children to do the same: writing the **a** in the air with their dominant hand.
- Give children paper and pencils or felt-tipped pens to practise writing the new grapheme.

> **Tip:** Make sure you repeat phonemes that can't be elongated such as **/a/**.

Practice

- Add the new letter card to the pile of letters children can read.
- Tell children they are going to read the letters they know.
- Show each card with the letter side facing them. If children can read the letter, move on.
- If children hesitate, show the picture side and quickly re-teach the image and the letter.

> Practice is vital so children can read the letters without hesitation.

70   © HarperCollins*Publishers* 2018

What to teach while reading Pink books

Phonics

Children will be able to move on to the Red A reading books with Phase 3 graphemes when they are able to read the graphemes in the box below and blend them into words with confidence.

> **j, v, w, x, y, z, zz, qu, ch, sh, th, ng, nk**

Review graphemes from Phase 2 that children find tricky. Typically, these are:

> **a, e, i, o, u, p, b, d, ck, ff, ll, ss**

For each book use the:
- phonic warm up to reinforce oral blending skills
- phonic activities to practise reading grapheme and words
- phonic activity sheet to practise the focus grapheme for the book you are reading.

Preparing for the Red books

- Continue to teach a sound a day, focusing on the Phase 3 graphemes for Red A. (See pages 6–7 for an example lesson plan.)
- Continue teaching word reading. (See page 68 for the steps in word reading.)
- Assess all Reception children once they have been taught all the Phase 2 phonemes. Use the assessment on pages 26–34 to place children at the appropriate band.
- Use the subsequent assessments every six weeks to ensure speedy progress.

Reading for pleasure

- Read aloud to children every day.
- Consider reading the *Reading for pleasure* books to enhance the *Big Cat Phonics for Letters and Sounds* book children are reading.
- Make connections between the books you read aloud to children and the *Big Cat Phonics for Letters and Sounds* books, so children see themselves as readers.
- Explain any unusual words in these books to help children grow their vocabulary.
- Return to well-loved books. Repeated reading helps children internalise these stories, which helps their comprehension and writing.

Research
- The volume of books read by or read to children has a direct impact on the size of their vocabulary.
- Children's books have a wider range of rare and rich vocabulary than adult conversation.
- Children will not meet this rare and rich vocabulary unless they read or are read to.
- Reading to children gives them a deeper vocabulary, a better understanding of how books work, and sets them up for success when they can read independently.

Anne E. Cunningham and Keith E. Stanovich, 'What Reading Does for the Mind', *Journal of Direct Instruction*, 2001

© HarperCollins*Publishers* 2018

Pat it

(Chant and Chatter Book 1)

Book band: Pink A

This book is about a visit to a farm, where the children see baby animals, play in the sand pit and watch the animals feeding.

Practising phonics Phase 2

Warm up: Follow me

- Say each sound of the animal names, asking children to repeat the sounds and then say the animal's name. (If children cannot blend the word themselves, say the sounds and then say the word.) Animals: **h/or/se, c/a/t, h/e/n, ch/i/ck, g/oa/t, l/a/mb, sh/ee/p**.

  New: Practise the sounds /s/ /a/ /t/ /p/ /i/ /n/

- Introduce the new sounds to prepare for reading Book 2 (see page 69).
- Make sure children are confident at reading these sounds.
- Use **Pat it: Resource sheet 1** to introduce the focus sound. Show children the image of the sun to help them link the grapheme to the phoneme. Ask children to say the sound as they trace the letter.

- Tell children to match the pictures to the focus sound: **/s/**.

Decoding practice

- Practise reading the words on the front page of the book.
- Ask children to complete the final activity on **Pat it: Resource sheet 1**. Tell them to say the sounds.

Children read

- Tell children to read the book aloud. Encourage them to sound out the words and explore the pictures.
- Listen to children as they read.
- When children have finished reading, ask them to find things on pages 14–15 that include the focus sound **/s/**.

After reading

Developing fluency

- Read each chant aloud, asking children to follow in their books.
  - Tell children to join in with you as you read.
  - Hesitate as you read so children can take over reading the next word.
- Tell children what you are thinking as you read so they can see how you make links between the words and the story, for example: *When I read 'pat pat', I think of the child gently patting the animals.*
- Ask children to read each chant with expression to a partner.
- Have fun with the chants, enjoy the rhythm and make up actions to bring them to life!

Comprehension

- Ask children to talk to their partner about the story. Would they like to go on a farm visit? What would they enjoy most? Take feedback.

- Talk about the names of baby animals. Look at pages 2 and 3 and talk about what baby sheep are called. Do children know the names of other farm animals?
- Look through the book and talk about the baby animals they see. Use **Pat it: Resource sheet 2** to match parent and baby animals.

Extending vocabulary

- Look back at each double page spread and discuss what is happening in the pictures. Encourage children to think about the movements the children and animals are making.
  - Act out the ways the animals move.
  - Help children link appropriate verbs to each animal. Ask: *Does a hen chew or peck? Does a lamb plod or frisk?*

Reading for pleasure

What the Ladybird Heard Julia Donaldson and Lydia Monks

Farmer Duck Martin Waddell

Where, Oh Where is Rosie's Chick? Pat Hutchins

A Visit to City Farm Verna Wilkins and Karin Littlewood

Pat it: Resource sheet 1
Phonic focus: /s/

Name: _____

Say the phoneme. Talk about the picture. Trace the grapheme.

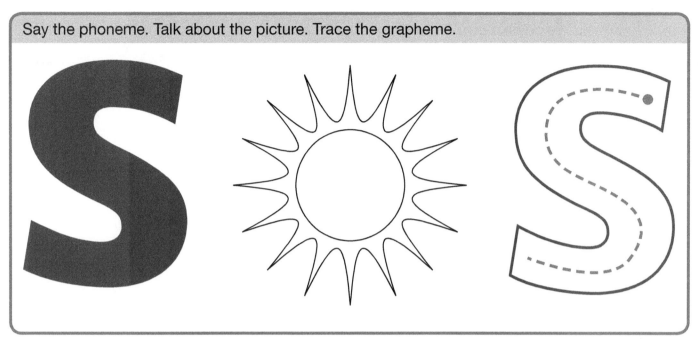

What begins with /s/? Circle the correct pictures.

What can you see? Say the sound /s/. Say the phoneme.

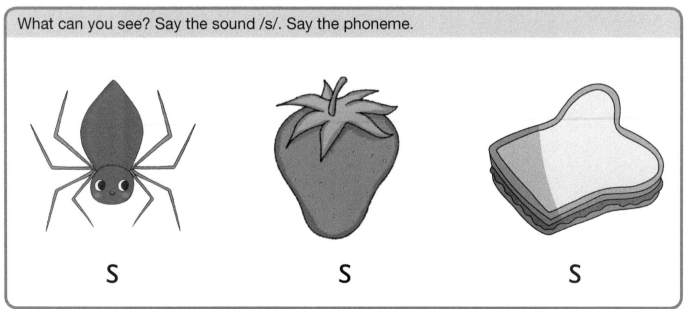

s   s   s

© HarperCollins*Publishers* 2018   Pink A: Pat it

Pat it: Resource sheet 2
Comprehension (Connecting) and Vocabulary

Name: _____

Which animals live on the farm? Circle the farm animals.

Draw a line to match the parent animal to its baby. Say the names of the baby farm animals.

74 Pink A: Pat it © HarperCollins*Publishers* 2018

Pit Pat

(Chant and Chatter Book 2)

Book band: Pink A

This book is about different types of weather. Children play in the rain and sun, and we see a rainbow.

Practising phonics Phase 2

Warm up: Simon says
- Play 'Simon says', sounding out the action you want children to do, for example: *Simon says j/u/m/p in the puddles; s/k/i/p in the sun* and so on.

  Review: /s/ /a/ /t/ /p/ /i/ /n/
- Make sure children are confident reading these sounds.
- Use **Pit Pat: Resource sheet 1** to introduce the focus sound. Show children the image of the apple to help them link the grapheme to the phoneme.
- Ask children to say the sound as they trace the letter.
- Tell children to match the pictures to the focus sound: **/a/**.

Decoding practice
- Practise reading the words on the front page of the book.
- Ask children to complete the final activity on **Pit Pat: Resource sheet 1**. Tell them to read the words.

Children read
- Tell children to read the book aloud. Encourage them to sound out the words and explore the pictures.
- Listen to children as they read.
- When children have finished reading, ask them to find things on pages 14–15 that include the focus sound **/a/**.

After reading

Developing fluency
- Help children gain fluency when reading. Read each chant aloud, asking them to follow in their books.
  - Tell children to join in with you as you read.
  - Hesitate as you read so children can take over reading the next word.
- Tell children what you are thinking as you read so they can see how you make links between the words and the story, for example: *When I read 'pit pat', it makes me think of the sound rain makes. I can hear the rain pit patting on the ground.*
- Read each chant with expression. Ask children to have a go at reading with expression to a partner.
- Have fun with the chants, enjoy the rhythm and make up actions to bring them to life!

Comprehension
- Ask children to talk to their partner about the weather in the book.
- Talk to children about appropriate clothing for going out in the sun and rain. Ask children to think about why the child on pages 10–11 is patting on sunscreen.
- Ask children if they have played in the rain. Have they ever jumped in puddles? What do they like about playing outside?

Extending vocabulary
- Talk about words that make sounds: onomatopoeia.
- Ask children if they can remember the sound the rain made: **pit pat**. Explain that you want to make a list of words that make sounds.
- Say: *splash* (with feeling), asking children to repeat the word. Explain that **splash** sounds like water going everywhere.
- Say: *splish splash*. Ask children to tell their partner what they think those words sound like.
- Teach children other onomatopoeic words such as: **pitter-patter**, **squelch**, **stomp** and so on.
- Encourage children to use the words throughout the day.

Reading for pleasure

Alfie Weather Shirley Hughes

The Wild Weather Book: Loads of things to do outdoors in rain, wind and snow Fiona Danks and Jo Schofield

Rosie's Hat Julia Donaldson

Bringing the Rain to Kapiti Plain Verna Aardema and Beatriz Vidal

© HarperCollins*Publishers* 2018

Pit Pat: Resource sheet 1
Phonic focus: /a/

Name: _____

Say the phoneme. Talk about the picture. Trace the grapheme.

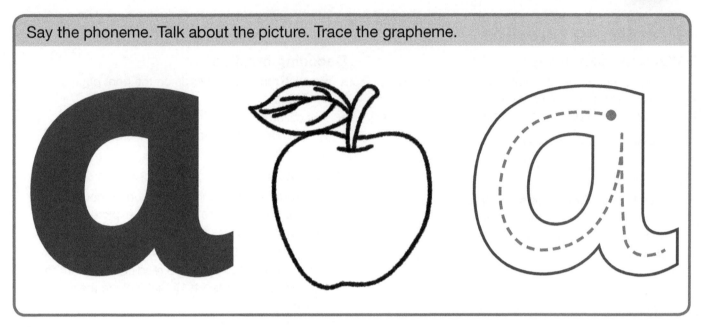

What begins with /a/? Circle the correct pictures.

Read the words.

tap   pan   nap

76   Pink A: Pit Pat

Pit Pat: Resource sheet 2
Comprehension (Connecting) and Vocabulary

Name: _____

Circle items you wear in the rain.

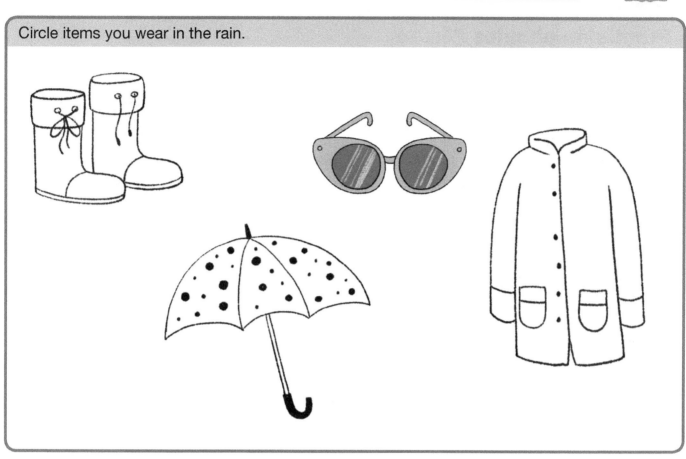

Talk about the different types of weather. Make weather sounds.

Pink A: Pit Pat 77

Sip it

(Chant and Chatter Book 3)

Book band: Pink A

In this non-fiction book we find out about how tea is grown, picked, transported and sold in shops.

Practising phonics Phase 2

Warm up: Sound buttons

- Write these words on cards: **in**, **it**, **at**, **am**, **sip** and **tin**.
- Show children a card. Say the word.
- Ask children to help you count the sounds in the word.
- Draw a dot beneath each sound. Say the dots show that the letter makes a sound. These are sound buttons.
- Ask children to read each sound and blend the word.
- Repeat for the other words.

> **New: Practise the sound /d/**

> **Focus: /n/ /d/**

> **Review: /s/ /a/ /t/ /p/ /i/ /n/**

- Introduce the new sounds to prepare for reading Book 7 (see page 69).
- Make sure children are confident reading these sounds.
- Use **Sip it: Resource sheet 1** to introduce the focus sounds. Show children the images of the nest and the dog to help them link the grapheme to the phoneme. Ask children to say the sound as they trace the letter.
- Tell children to match the pictures to the focus sounds: **/n/** and **/d/**.

Decoding practice

- Practise reading the words on the front page of the book.
- Ask children to complete the final activity on **Sip it: Resource sheet 1**. Tell them to read the words.

Children read

- Tell children to read the book aloud. Encourage them to sound out the words and explore the pictures.
- Listen to children as they read.
- When children have finished reading, ask them to find things on pages 14–15 that include the focus sounds **/n/** and **/d/**.

After reading

Developing fluency

- Help children gain fluency when reading. Read each chant aloud, asking them to follow in their books.
  - Tell children to join in with you as you read.
  - Hesitate as you read so children can take over reading the next word.
- Tell children what you are thinking as you read so they can see how you make links between the words and the story, for example: *On page 2 the sentence 'Nip at a tip' helps me understand the picture. I can see that the tea pickers are nipping at the tea leaves with their fingers.*
- Read each chant with expression and ask children to have a go at reading with expression to a partner.
- Have fun with the chants, enjoy the rhythm and make up actions to bring them to life!

Comprehension

- Children talk about the book. Have they tried a drink of tea? What do they know about tea?

- Go back through the book and use sequencing words and phrases to tell the story of tea, for example: *First the tea pickers nip the tips of the tea leaves. Then …*
- Ask children to tell the story of tea to their partner as they look through the book.

Extending vocabulary

What food tastes like

- Cut up a variety of fruits for children to taste.
- Ask children to eat each piece of fruit slowly and think about what it tastes like. Explain that everyone tastes differently.
- Play 'Which one?':
  - Ask: *How sweet was the fruit? Was it* **as sweet as sugar** *or* **fresh and zesty**?
  - Repeat with each piece of fruit. Help children to describe what they taste by giving them different choices each time, for example: **sour as a lemon** or **mouth-watering**; **juicy and sweet** or **strong and bitter**.

Reading for pleasure

How Did That Get in My Lunchbox? Chris Butterworth

Juliana's Bananas: Where do your bananas come from? Ruth Walton

Eat Your Greens, Goldilocks Steve Smallman and Bruno Robert

Tasty Poems Jill Bennett and Nick Sharratt

Sip it: Resource sheet 1
Phonic focus: /n/ and /d/

Name: _____

Say the phoneme. Talk about the picture. Trace the grapheme.

What begins with /n/? Circle the correct picture.

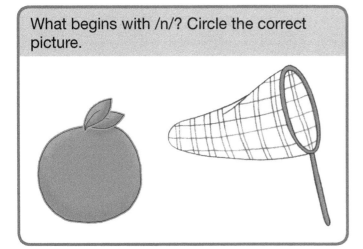

What begins with /d/? Circle the correct picture.

Read the words.

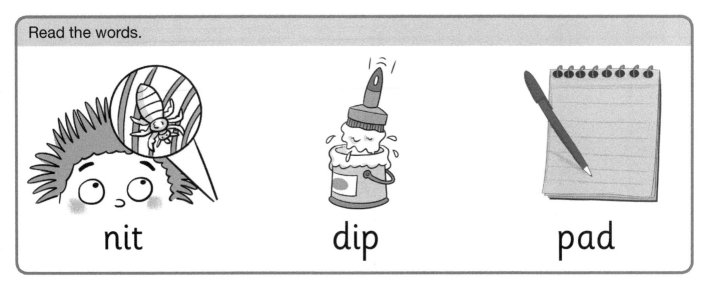

nit   dip   pad

© HarperCollins*Publishers* 2018   Pink A: Sip it   79

Sip it: Resource sheet 2
Comprehension (Sequencing) and Vocabulary

Name: _____

Sequence the journey of tea from bush to cup, using the pictures.

What words can you think of that mean hot? For example: very warm, boiling, roasting, scorching, sweltering, blistering, humid. Say the words.

Map Man

(Chant and Chatter Book 4)

Book band: Pink A

This book is about Map Man, a superhero with amazing mapping skills. He zooms in and can see when people or animals need help.

Practising phonics Phase 2

Warm up: What's in the box?
- Hide some objects in a box: map, pin, man, mat.
- Tell children they must work out what is in the box.
- Display the letters of the word. Put them out in order, for example: **m-a-p**. Ask children to read the letters and blend them.
- Say the sounds of the word as you point to each letter, for example: **m/a/p**. Ask children to shout out the answer to: *What's in the box?*
- Say the sounds of the word again. Ask children to repeat the sounds and then say the word.
- Show children the object/picture in the box.
- Repeat for other objects.

> New: Practise the sound /m/
>
> Focus: /p/
>
> Review: /s/ /a/ /t/ /p/ /i/ /n/ /d/

- Introduce the new sound (see page 69).
- Make sure children are confident reading these sounds.
- Use **Map Man: Resource sheet 1** to introduce the focus sound. Show children the image of the pan to help them link the grapheme to the phoneme. Ask children to say the sound as they trace the letter.
- Tell children to match the pictures to the focus sound: /p/.

Decoding practice
- Practise reading the words on the front page of the book.
- Ask children to complete the final activity on **Map Man: Resource sheet 1**. Tell them to read the words.

Children read
- Tell children to read the book aloud. Encourage them to sound out the words and explore the pictures.
- Listen to children as they read.
- When children have finished reading, ask them to find things on pages 14–15 that include the focus sound /p/.

After reading

Developing fluency
- Help children gain fluency when reading. Read each chant aloud, asking them to follow in their books.
  - Tell children to join in with you as you read.
  - Hesitate as you read so children can take over reading the next word.
- Tell children what you are thinking as you read so they can see how you make links between the words and the story, for example: *When I read 'dip, dip, dip', I can see that Map Man is diving deeper and deeper under the water. He is going to save the toy robot. I am going to say that with feeling so it sounds exciting!*
- Read each chant with expression. Ask children to have a go at reading with expression to a partner.
- Have fun with the chants, enjoy the rhythm and make up actions to bring them to life!

Comprehension
- Ask children to talk to their partner about superheroes. What do they do? Which superheroes have they heard of?
- Retell Map Man's adventures. Can children remember the three things he rescues? (cat, dog, toy robot)
- Ask children to discuss each of Map Map's rescues. Which words would they use to describe Map Man? Go through the book discussing the pictures and write a list of adjectives that describe Map Man.

Extending vocabulary
- Ask children what they would do if they were a superhero. What powers would they like to have?
- Help children to extend their ideas using **because** or **so**. Give them sentence stems such as: *I would like to fly,* **so** *...* or *It would be amazing to have super strength,* **because** *...*

Reading for pleasure

Traction Man is Here Mini Grey

Supertato Sue Hendra

Stuck Oliver Jeffers

Amelia Earhart Ma Isabel Sanchez Vegara and Mariadiamantes

© HarperCollins*Publishers* 2018

Map Man: Resource sheet 1
Phonic focus: /p/

Name: _____

Say the phoneme. Talk about the picture. Trace the grapheme.

What begins with /p/? Circle the correct pictures.

Read the words.

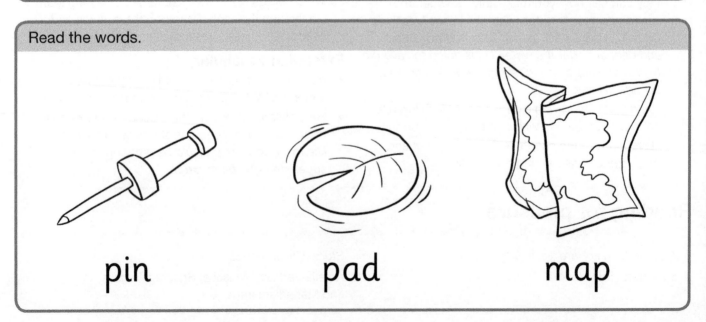

pin   pad   map

82   Pink A: Map Man   © HarperCollins*Publishers* 2018

Map Man: Resource sheet 2
Comprehension (Retelling) and Vocabulary

Name: _____

Retell the story of Map Man.

What words would you use to describe Map Man? Colour in the picture.

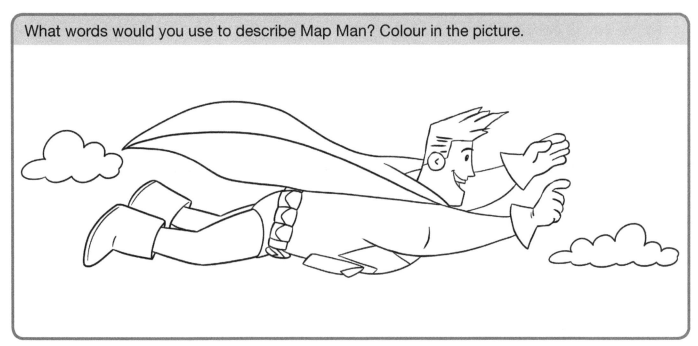

Pip Pip Pip

(Chant and Chatter Book 5)

Book band: Pink A

This book is about some villagers who give a man their last apple. He gives the pips to a child, who plants them. Eventually, the pips grow into apple trees, whose fruit the whole village enjoys.

Practising phonics Phase 2

Warm up: Say the sounds
- You will need pictures/objects of one-syllable words, for example: **duck**, **pip**, **tree**, **cup**, **man**, **cat**, **rain**.
- Pair children into 'teacher' and 'pupil'.
  - Give the 'teacher' an object/picture.
  - The 'teacher' says the sounds of the word.
  - The 'pupil' repeats the sounds and blends them to say the word.
  - The 'teacher' shows the object/picture. Was the 'pupil' correct?
  - Swap roles, giving out new objects/pictures.

Focus: /i/ /m/

Review: /s/ /a/ /t/ /p/ /i/ /n/ /m/ /d/

- Make sure children are confident reading these sounds.
- Use **Pip Pip Pip: Resource sheet 1** to introduce the focus sounds. Show children the images of an insect and a mouse to help them link the grapheme to the phoneme. Ask children to say the sound as they trace the letter.
- Tell children to match the pictures to the focus sounds: **/i/** and **/m/**.

Decoding practice
- Practise reading the words on the front page of the book.
- Ask children to complete the final activity on **Pip Pip Pip: Resource sheet 1**. Tell them to read the words.

Children read
- Tell children to read the book aloud. Encourage them to sound out the words and explore the pictures.
- Listen to children as they read.
- When children have finished reading, ask them to find things on pages 14–15 that include the focus sounds **/i/** and **/m/**.

After reading

Developing fluency
- Read each chant aloud, asking children to follow in their books.
  - Tell children to join in with you as you read.
  - Hesitate as you read so children can take over reading the next word.
- Tell children what you are thinking as you read so they can see how you make links between the words and the story, for example: *When I read 'a man did it', I think about how amazing it is that tiny pips have become beautiful trees hanging with fruit. I will say it with feeling to show how amazing it is: A man did it!*
- Read each chant with expression and ask children to have a go at reading with expression to a partner.
- Have fun with the chants, enjoy the rhythm and make up actions to bring them to life!

Comprehension
- Children talk about the story. Can they tell their partner about what happened to the pips?

- Say: *At the end of the story is says 'A man did it'. But everyone in the village helped! Can you name any other stories where the characters helped each other?*
- Ask children if they have ever planted a seed. What happened?

Extending vocabulary
- Look at the pages where the apple pips are planted and talk about how the tiny pips have grown into huge trees.
- Say the words: *tiny, miniature* and *little*. Discuss which word would be the best word to describe the apple pips.
- Say the words: *huge, enormous* and *giant*. Discuss which word would be best to describe the apple trees.
- Say the sentence: *The pips were _____ but they grew into _____ trees.* Ask children to help you choose the best words. Can they think of any other words they could use?

Reading for pleasure

The Elves and the Shoemaker

The Enormous Turnip

The Lion Inside Rachel Bright and Jim Field

The Smartest Giant in Town Julia Donaldson and Axel Scheffler

The Crow's Tale Naomi Howarth

Pip Pip Pip: Resource sheet 1
Phonic focus: /i/ and /m/

Name: _____

Say the phoneme. Talk about the picture. Trace the grapheme.

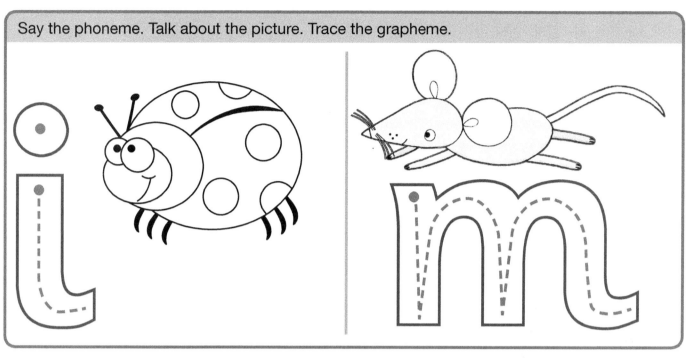

What begins with /i/?
Circle the correct picture.

What begins with /m/?
Circle the correct picture.

Read the words.

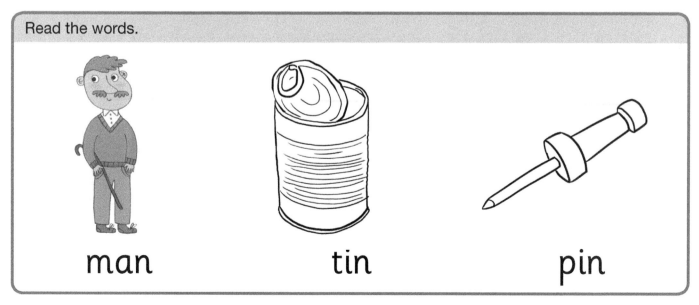

man　　　　　　　tin　　　　　　　pin

© HarperCollins*Publishers* 2018　　　　　　　Pink A: Pip Pip Pip

Pip Pip Pip: Resource sheet 2
Comprehension (Character) and Vocabulary

Name: _____

How is the man in the story feeling in these pictures?

What words can you think of that mean happy? For example: cheerful, overjoyed, jolly, delighted, content, joyful, ecstatic. Talk about the pictures.

86   Pink A: Pip Pip Pip   © HarperCollins*Publishers* 2018

Tip it

(Chant and Chatter Book 6)

Book band: Pink A

This book is about a family recycling unwanted objects. Later they find their recycling has been made into wonderful new things and is on display in a shop.

Practising phonics Phase 2

Warm up: What's in the box?
- Hide some pictures/objects in a box.
- Say the sounds of an object, for example: **f/o/x**. Ask children to shout out the answer to: *What's in the box?*
- Say the sounds of the word again. Ask children to repeat the sounds and then say the word.
- Repeat for other objects.

  New: Practise the sounds /g/ /o/

  Focus: /t/

  Review: /a/ /t/ /p/ /i/ /n/ /m/ /d/

- Introduce the new sounds (see page 69).
- Make sure children are confident reading all the sounds.
- Use **Tip it: Resource sheet 1** to introduce the focus sound. Show children the image of the spinning top to help them link the grapheme to the phoneme. Ask children to say the sound as they trace the letter.
- Tell children to match the pictures to the focus sound: **/t/**.

Decoding practice
- Practise reading the words on the front page of the book.
- Ask children to complete the final activity on **Tip it: Resource sheet 1**. Tell them to read the words.

Children read
- Tell children to read the book aloud. Encourage them to sound out the words and explore the pictures.
- Listen to children as they read.
- When children have finished reading, ask them to find things on pages 14–15 that include the focus sound **/t/**.

After reading

Developing fluency
- Help children gain fluency when reading. Read each chant aloud, asking them to follow in their books.
  - Tell children to join in with you as you read.
  - Hesitate as you read so children can take over reading the next word.
- Tell children what you are thinking as you read so they can see how you make links between the words and the story, for example: *When I read the labels, I know that each label tells me what that object is. It really helps me.*
- Read each chant with expression. Ask children to have a go at reading with expression to a partner.
- Have fun with the chants, enjoy the rhythm and make up actions to bring them to life!

Comprehension
- Ask children to talk to their partner about recycling. Have they ever made anything from old unwanted things?
- Draw children's attention to the pages with labels. Explain that labels are a feature of a fact book.
- Look at the final page. Can children see some of the items the family recycled?
- Ask children to practise writing labels on **Tip it: Resource sheet 2**. Remind them how to say the word and segment it into sounds. Tell them to write each sound in order.

Extending vocabulary
- Show children some old objects. Ask them what they think these objects were used for. Take feedback.
- Describe the objects using adjectives, for example: *This is dusty, the paint is peeling, it is red and green* and so on. Can children work out which object you are describing?
- Ask children to describe an object to their partner using adjectives.

Reading for pleasure

Tidy Emily Gravett

Recycling Things to Make and Do Emily Bone and Leonie Pratt

The Tin Forest Helen Ward and Wayne Anderson

Dinosaurs and All That Rubbish Michael Foreman

Stories for a Fragile Planet Kenneth Steven and Jane Ray

Tip it: Resource sheet 1
Phonic focus: /t/

Name: _____

Say the phoneme. Talk about the picture. Trace the grapheme.

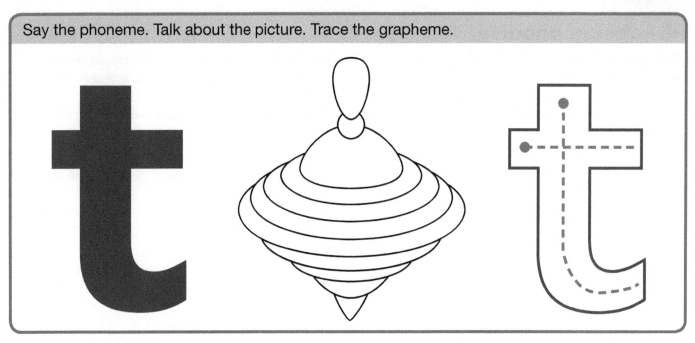

What begins with /t/? Circle the correct pictures.

Read the words.

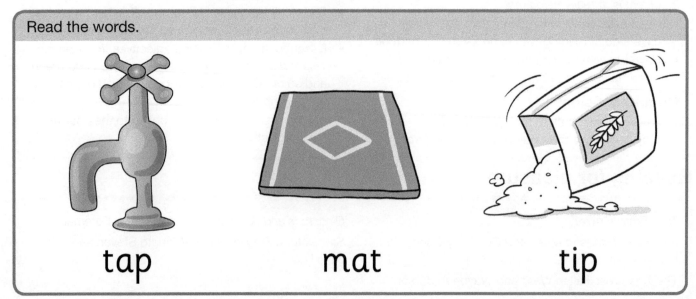

tap   mat   tip

Tip it: Resource sheet 2
Comprehension (Recalling) and Vocabulary

Name: _____

Circle the items that the family recycled.

Describe the objects upcycled from the story. Talk about the objects. Which is your favourite object?

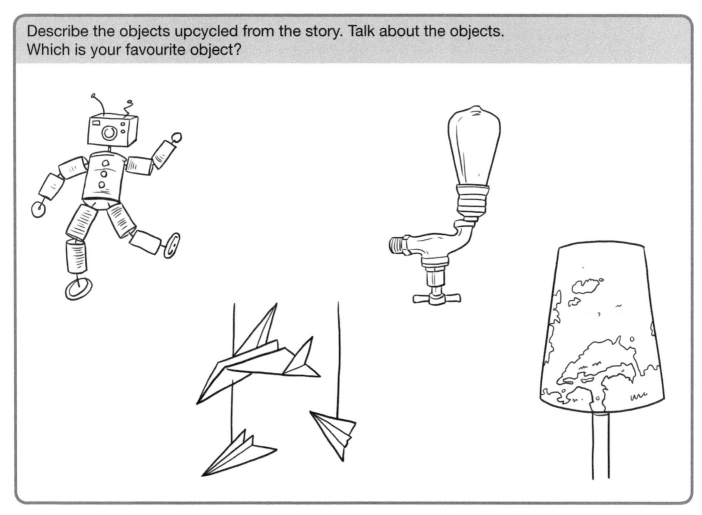

© HarperCollins*Publishers* 2018   Pink A: Tip it   89

Dig it

(Chant and Chatter Book 7)

Book band: Pink B

This book is about a dad, a child and a dog all having fun at their allotment.

Practising phonics Phase 2

Warm up: What's in the box?
- Hide some objects/pictures in a box: dog, dig, mat, map, dad.
- Ask children to work out what is in the box.
- Display the letters of the word. Put them out in order, for example: **d-o-g**. Ask children to read the letters and blend them.
- Say the sounds of the word as you point to each letter, for example: **d/o/g**. Ask children to shout out the answer to: *What's in the box?* (Miss out this step if children are confident at reading and blending.)
- Repeat for other objects.

> New: Practise the sounds /c/ /k/ /ck/

> Focus: /g/ /o/

> Review: /s/ /a/ /t/ /p/ /i/ /n/ /m/ /d/

- Introduce the new sounds to prepare for reading Book 8 (see page 69). Teach children that the digraph **/ck/** is two letters that make one sound.
- Make sure children are confident reading these sounds.
- Use **Dig it: Resource sheet 1** to introduce the focus sound. Show children the images of the gate and the octopus to help them link the grapheme to the phoneme. Ask children to say the sound as they trace the letter.
- Tell children to match the pictures to the focus sounds: **/g/** and **/o/**.

Decoding practice
- Show children how you mark the digraph **/ck/** in a word such as **pick** with a line beneath it rather than a sound button. Read some words with the **/ck/** digraph: **lick**, **pick**, **tick**, **lock** and **sock**.
- Practise reading the words on the front page of the book.
- Ask children to complete the final activity on **Dig it: Resource sheet 1**. Tell them to read the words.

Children read
- Tell children to read the book aloud. Encourage them to sound out the words and explore the pictures.
- Listen to children as they read.
- When children have finished reading, ask them to find things on pages 14–15 that include the focus sounds **/g/** and **/o/**.

After reading

Developing fluency
- Help children gain fluency when reading. Read each chant aloud, asking them to follow in their books.
  - Tell children to join in with you as you read.
  - Hesitate as you read so children can take over reading the next word.
- Tell children what you are thinking as you read so they can see how you make links between the words and the story, for example: *When I read 'Pop it on top', I can see the child is speaking* – show children the speech bubble. *So I am going to say 'Pop it on top' as if I am telling Dad what to do.*
- Read each chant with expression and ask children to have a go at reading with expression to a partner.
- Have fun with the chants, enjoy the rhythm and make up actions to bring them to life!

Comprehension
- Ask children to talk to their partner about gardening. Have they ever grown anything?
- Talk about the jobs Dad and the child are doing. Make labels together to describe each job, for example, pages 6–7: 'Dig it' and 'Pop it in the pit'.

Extending vocabulary
- Tell children gardening can be hard work. Play 'Show me':
  - Show children what it looks like when you are tired: slump and sigh a bit.
  - Ask children: *Show me tired – move as if you are tired.* Feed back what they are doing that shows tiredness, for example: *When you drag your feet I can see how tired you are!*
  - Repeat for: **excited**, **grumpy** and **shy**.

Reading for pleasure

Eddie's Garden Sarah Garland
Yucky Worms Vivian French

The Curious Garden Peter Brown
The Tiny Seed Eric Carle

Dig it: Resource sheet 1
Phonic focus: /g/ and /o/

Name: _____

Say the phoneme. Talk about the picture. Trace the grapheme.

What begins with /g/? Circle the correct picture.

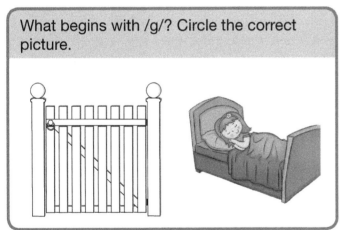

What begins with /o/? Circle the correct picture.

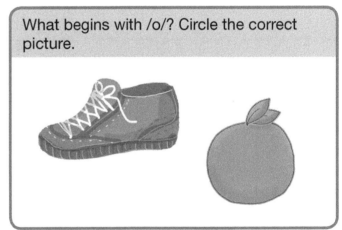

Read the words.

dig   dog   mog

© HarperCollins*Publishers* 2018 — Pink B: Dig it

Dig it: Resource sheet 2
Comprehension (Connecting) and Vocabulary

Name: _____

What things might you use when gardening? Circle the correct items.

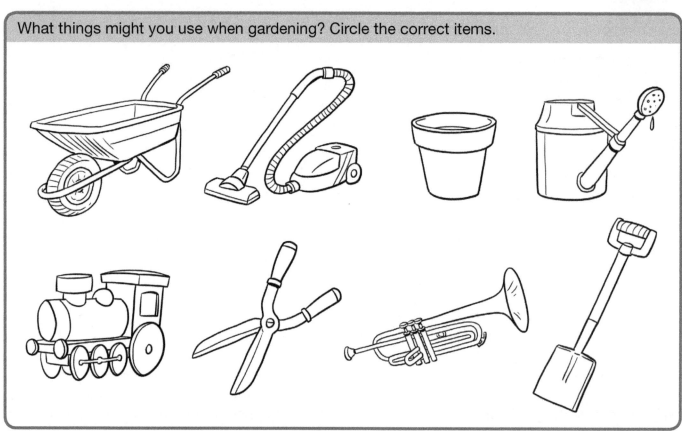

What words describe the plant? For example: tall, runner bean, leafy, lush, bushy, green, fertile. Talk about the picture and colour it in.

Not a Pot

(Chant and Chatter Book 8)

Book band: Pink B

This book is about a little boy and girl going on a garden hunt. They have to follow a map and dig items up. The little girl, Kim, successfully digs up a pot. Will Nick dig up a pot too?

Practising phonics Phase 2

Warm up: Reading words with the digraph ck

- Write these words on cards: **pick**, **tick**, **kick**, **sack**, **sock**. Show children a card. Say the word.
- Ask children to help you count the sounds in the word.
- Draw a dot beneath each sound and a line beneath the digraph **/ck/**. Explain that dots show the letter makes a sound. These are sound buttons. The line shows that two letters are making one sound.
- Ask children to read each sound and blend the word.
- Repeat for the other words.

> New: Practise the sounds /e/ /u/

> Focus: /c/ /k/ /ck/

> Review: /s/ /a/ /t/ /p/ /i/ /n/ /m/ /d/ /g/ /o/

- Introduce the new sounds to prepare for reading Book 9 (see page 69).
- Make sure children are confident reading these sounds.

- Use **Not a Pot: Resource sheet 1** to introduce the focus sound. Show children the images of the cake, kettle and sack to help them link the grapheme to the phoneme. Ask children to say the sound as they trace the letter.
- Tell children to match the pictures to the focus graphemes: **c**, **k** and **ck**.

Decoding practice

- Practise reading the words on the front page of the book.
- Children complete the final activity on **Not a Pot: Resource sheet 1**. Tell them to read the words.

Children read

- Tell children to read the book aloud. Encourage them to sound out the words and explore the pictures.
- Listen to children as they read.
- When children have finished reading, ask them to find things on pages 14–15 that include the focus sounds **/c/**, **/k/** or **/ck/**.

After reading

Developing fluency

- Help children gain fluency when reading. Read each chant aloud, asking them to follow in their books.
  - Tell children to join in with you as you read.
  - Hesitate as you read so children can take over reading the next word.
- Tell children what you are thinking as you read so they can see how you make links between the words and the story, for example: *When I read 'Can Nick dig a pot?', I can see it's a question because of the question mark at the end of the sentence.*
- Read each chant with expression and ask children to have a go at reading with expression to a partner.
- Have fun with the chants, enjoy the rhythm and make up actions to bring them to life!

Comprehension

- Children talk to their partner about what they know about treasure hunts. Have they been on one?

- Use sequencing words and phrases to help order the events of the story. For example: *First, the children got a map. Then they packed the backpack with everything they needed.*
- Ask children to retell the story with their partner. Listen for children using sequencing words and phrases.

Extending vocabulary

Words to describe feelings

- Ask children to show you a surprised face. Describe what you can see: *When you are surprised you have huge eyes and I can see your mouths open wide!*
- Repeat for: **excited**, **disappointed** and **delighted**. If necessary, explain the word, for example: *When you open a present and you already have it you might be disappointed.*
- Ask which emotion the children in the book are feeling on each page.

Reading for pleasure

Captain Flinn and the Pirate Dinosaurs: Missing Treasure! Giles Andreae

The Runaway Dinner Allan Ahlberg

Snail Trail Ruth Brown

© HarperCollins*Publishers* 2018

Not a Pot: Resource sheet 1
Phonic focus: /c/, /k/ and /ck/

Name: _____

Say the phoneme. Talk about the picture. Trace the grapheme.

Read the words. What begins with /c/? Circle the correct pictures. Talk about the pictures.

 cat   dog   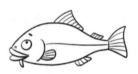 cod

Read the words. What begins with /k/? Circle the correct pictures. Talk about the pictures.

 kid    kick   pot

Read the words. What ends with /ck/? Circle the correct pictures. Talk about the pictures.

 sock   tap   sack

Not a Pot: Resource sheet 2
Comprehension (Sequencing) and Vocabulary

Name: _____

Can you recall the story and sequence the events below? Use the pictures to tell the story.

Use a range of words to describe how Nick and Kim are feeling below. What words describe Kim? For example: happy, excited, pleased, delighted, proud. What words describe Nick? For example: disappointed, unhappy, frustrated, cross.

© HarperCollins*Publishers* 2018   Pink B: Not a Pot   95

Pop Pop Pop! (Chant and Chatter Book 9)

Book band: Pink B

This book is based on the traditional tale *The Magic Porridge Pot*. In this version of the tale, a bear family have a magic popcorn pot!

Practising phonics Phase 2

Warm up: What's in the box?
- Hide some objects/pictures in a box: duck, rock, pan, sack, net.
- Ask children to work out what is in the box.
- Display the letters of the word. Put them out in order, for example: **d-u-ck**. Ask children read the letters and blend them.
- Say the sounds of the word as you point to each letter, for example: **d/u/ck**. Ask children to shout out the answer to: *What's in the box?* (Miss out this step if children are confident at reading and blending.) Repeat for other objects.

> New: Practise the sounds /r/ /h/

> Focus: /e/ /u/

> Review: /s/ /a/ /t/ /p/ /i/ /n/ /m/ /d/ /g/ /o/ /c/ /k/ /ck/

- Introduce the new sounds to prepare for reading Book 10 (see page 69). Make sure children are confident reading these sounds.
- Use **Pop Pop Pop!: Resource sheet 1** to introduce the focus sound. Show children the images of the egg and the umbrella to help them link the grapheme to the phoneme. Ask children to say the sound as they trace the letter.
- Tell children to match the pictures to the focus sounds: /e/ and /u/.

Decoding practice
- Practise reading the words on the front page of the book.
- Ask children to complete the final activity on **Pop Pop Pop!: Resource sheet 1**. Tell them to read the words.

Children read
- Tell children to read the book aloud. Encourage them to sound out the words and explore the pictures.
- Listen to children as they read.
- When children have finished reading, ask them to find things on pages 14–15 that include the focus sounds /e/ and /u/.

After reading

Developing fluency
- Help children gain fluency when reading. Read each chant aloud and ask them to follow in their books.
  - Tell children to join in with you as you read.
  - Hesitate as you read so children can take over reading the next word.
- Tell children what you are thinking as you read so they can see how you make links between the words and the story, for example: *When I read 'Pop pop pop', I know it is the sound of the popcorn popping. I can hear it going pop!* Ask children to say 'Pop!' as a sound effect with you.
- Read each chant with expression and ask children to have a go at reading with expression to a partner.

Comprehension
- Ask children to talk to their partner about the story. Did they think the popcorn would ever stop popping? What could have happened if Mum hadn't been able to stop the pot?
- Talk about the events in the story. Use **Pop Pop Pop!: Resource sheet 2** to sequence the story together. Ask children to work with their partner to sequence the story.

Extending vocabulary
- Ask children to talk about how they think Ted felt at the beginning of the story. Take feedback. Help children extend their vocabulary by offering better word choices, for example, **excited**, **hopeful**, **eager**.
- Ask children to talk about how they think Ted felt as the popcorn pile got deeper and deeper. Take feedback. Help children extend their vocabulary by offering better word choices, for example, **despairing**, **terrified**, **in shock**, **in a panic**.
- Model composing sentences: *At first Ted was _____ but then he felt_____.*
- Ask children to compose their own version of the sentence with their partner.

Reading for pleasure

The Witch with an Itch Helen Baugh
The Most Magnificent Thing Ashley Spires

Ada Twist, Scientist Andrea Beaty

Pop Pop Pop!: Resource sheet 1
Phonic focus: /e/ and /u/

Name: _____

Say the phoneme. Talk about the picture. Trace the grapheme.

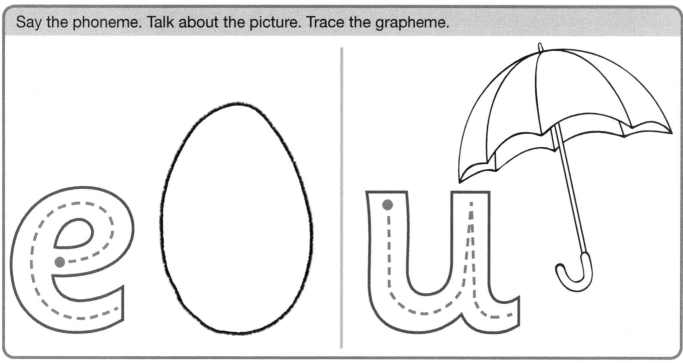

What begins with /e/? Circle the correct picture.

What begins with /u/? Circle the correct picture.

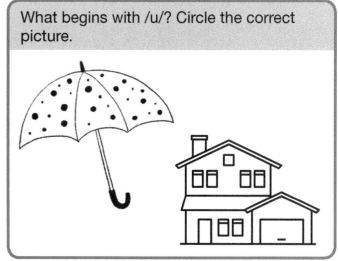

Read the words.

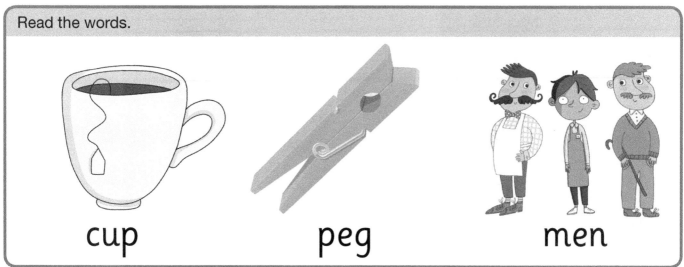

cup   peg   men

© HarperCollins*Publishers* 2018   Pink B: Pop Pop Pop!   97

Pop Pop Pop!: Resource sheet 2
Comprehension (Retelling) and Vocabulary

Name: _____

Use the story map to retell the story. Talk about how Ted feels through the story.

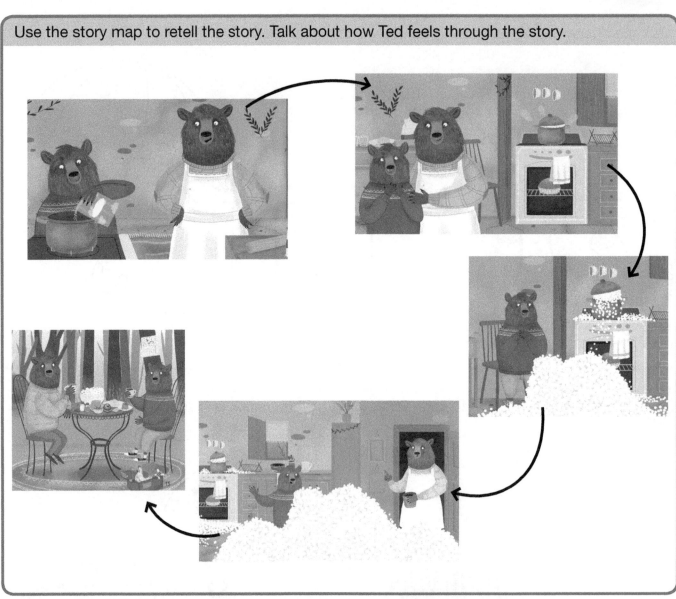

Use a range of words to describe how Ted feels through the story.

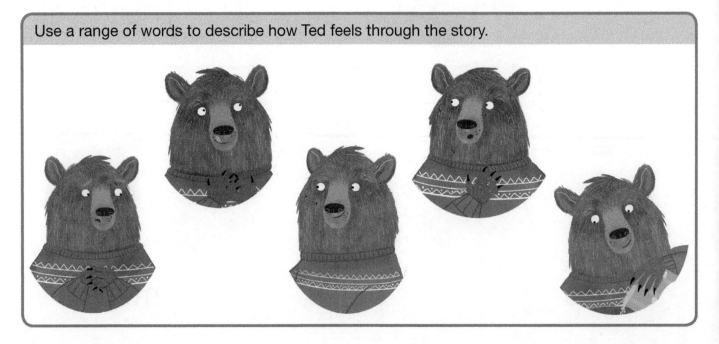

Pink B: Pop Pop Pop! © HarperCollins*Publishers* 2018

Up on Deck

(Chant and Chatter Book 10)

Book band: Pink B

This non-fiction book explores what you can see on a boat trip in spring.

Practising Phonics Phase 2

Warm up: Reading high frequency words
- Write these words on cards: **it, in, up, am, at, dad, can, get, not, mum**.
- Ask children to help you put sound buttons on the words (one button under each sound).
- Ask children to read the words independently: put your finger underneath each sound so they know which letter to read.

> New: Practise the sounds /b/ /f/ /ff/

> Focus: /r/ /h/

> Review: /s/ /a/ /t/ /p/ /i/ /n/ /m/ /d/ /g/ /o/ /c/ /k/ /ck/ /e/ /u/

- Introduce the new sounds to prepare for reading Book 11 (see page 69).
- Make sure children are confident reading these sounds.
- Use **Up on Deck: Resource sheet 1** to introduce the focus sounds. Show children the images of the rainbow and the horse to help them link the graphemes to the phonemes. Ask children to say the sound as they trace the letter.
- Tell children to match the pictures to the focus sounds: **/r/** and **/h/**.

Decoding practice
- Practise reading the words on the front page of the book.
- Ask children to complete the final activity on **Up on Deck: Resource sheet 1**. Tell them to read the words.

Children read
- Tell children to read the book aloud. Encourage them to sound out the words and explore the pictures.
- Listen to children as they read.
- When children have finished reading, ask them to find things on pages 14–15 that include the focus sounds /r/ and /h/.

After reading

Developing fluency
- Read each chant aloud and ask children to follow in their books.
  - Tell children to join in with you as you read.
  - Hesitate as you read so children can take over reading the next word.
- Tell children what you are thinking as you read so they can see how you make links between the words and the story, for example: *When I read 'A duck sits and pecks', it makes me think about what the duck is doing. I really like the word 'pecks' because it is a special word to describe how birds use their beaks.*
- Read each chant with expression and ask children to have a go at reading with expression to a partner.
- Have fun with the chants, enjoy the rhythm and make up actions to bring them to life!

Comprehension
- Ask children to talk to their partner about the book. Have they ever been on a boat or visited a river? Take feedback.
- Draw children's attention to pages 10–13. Discuss what the duck is doing. Ask children to look closely at the nest. Can they count the eggs? Talk about how the ducklings hatch from the eggs.
- Ask children to look back through the book and look for the other animals in the book. Help them read the words **pup** and **rat**, and link these to the pictures.

Extending vocabulary
- Remind children that a baby duck is called a duckling and that a duckling hatches from an egg.
- Ask children to look at the animal on pages 6–7. Can they remember the special word for a baby dog?
- Ask children to think of all the animals they know.
- Work together to make a list of the proper names of baby animals.

Reading for pleasure

Mr Gumpy's Outing John Burningham
The River: An Epic Journey to the Sea Patricia Hegarty
Hop Aboard! Here We Go! Richard Scarry
First Book of Ships and Boats Isabel Thomas
Little Tim and the Brave Sea Captain Edward Ardizzone

© HarperCollins*Publishers* 2018

Up on Deck: Resource sheet 1
Phonic focus: /r/ and /h/

Name: _____

Say the phoneme. Talk about the picture. Trace the grapheme.

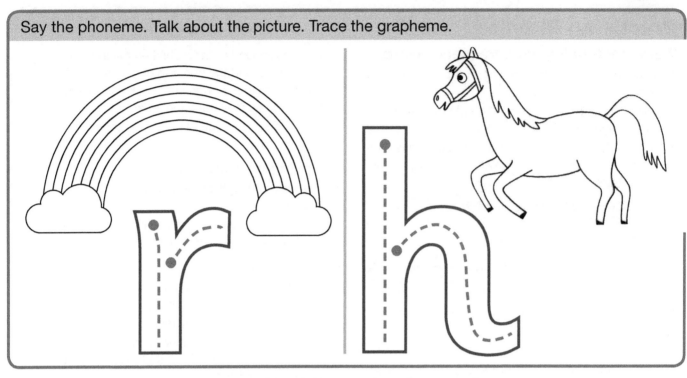

What begins with /r/? Circle the correct picture.

What begins with /h/? Circle the correct picture.

Read the words.

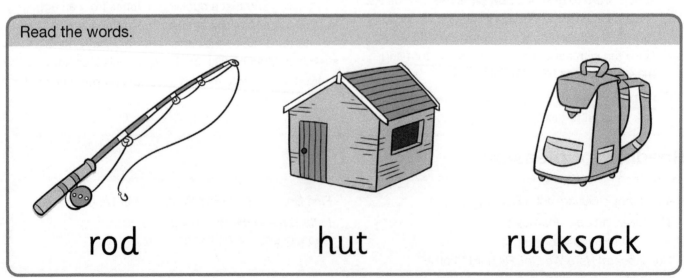

rod	hut	rucksack

Up on Deck: Resource sheet 2
Comprehension (Predicting)

Name: _____

Talk about what has happened in the book. Look at the pictures and make predictions.

What words could you use to describe the animals? Which is your favourite animal and why?

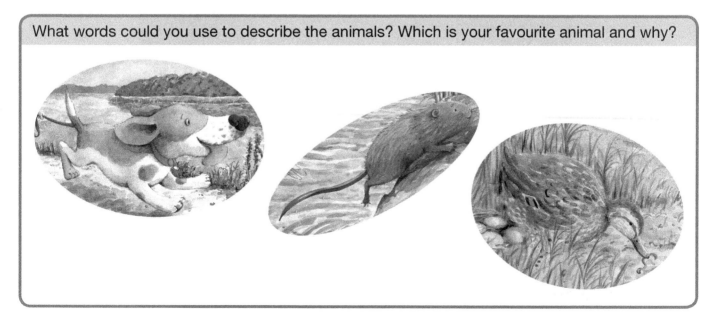

© HarperCollins*Publishers* 2018   Pink B: Up on Deck

Mog and Mim (Chant and Chatter Book 11)

Book band: Pink B

This book is about two aliens, Mog and Mim, who are having a race across their planet. Mim is not as fearless as Mog and soon falls behind. When Mim has a tumble, Mog saves the day by helping Mim.

Practising phonics Phase 2

Warm up: Reading words with the digraphs: /ck/, /ll/, /ff/, /ss/

- Write these words on cards: **back**, **off**, **hill**, **fell**, **mess**, **miss**.
- Show children a card. Say the word. Ask children to help you count the sounds in the word.
- Draw a dot beneath each sound and a line beneath the digraph **/ff/** in **off**. Explain the dots show that the letter makes a sound. These are sound buttons. The line shows that two letters are making one sound.
- Ask children to read each sound and blend the word.
- Repeat for the other words.

> New: Practise the sounds /l/ /ll/ /ss/

> Focus: /b/ /f/ /ff/

> Review: /s/ /a/ /t/ /p/ /i/ /n/ /m/ /d/ /g/ /o/ /c/ /k/ /ck/ /e/ /u/

- Introduce the new sounds to prepare for reading Book 12 (see page 69).
- Make sure children are confident reading these sounds.
- Use **Mog and Mim: Resource sheet 1** to introduce the focus sounds. Show children the images of the ball, fish and Mog (huffing and puffing) to help them link the grapheme to the phoneme. Ask children to say the sound as they trace the letter.
- Tell children to match the pictures to the focus sounds: **/b/**, **/f/** and **/ff/**.

Decoding practice

- Practise reading the words on the front page of the book.
- Ask children to complete the final activity on **Mog and Mim: Resource sheet 1**. Tell them to read the words.

Children read

- Tell children to read the book aloud. Encourage them to sound out the words and explore the pictures.
- Listen to children as they read.
- When children have finished reading, ask them to find things on pages 14–15 that include the focus sounds **/b/**, **/f/** and **/ff/**.

After reading

Developing fluency

- Help children gain fluency when reading. Read each chant aloud and ask them to follow in their books.
  - Tell children to join in with you as you read.
  - Hesitate as you read so children can take over reading the next word.
- Tell children what you are thinking as you read so they can see how you make links between the words and the story, for example: *When I read 'Mog hops up and off', I think Mog is excited about running down the crater. She isn't afraid at all.*
- Read each chant with expression and ask children to have a go at reading with expression to a partner.
- Have fun with the chants, enjoy the rhythm and make up actions to bring them to life!

Comprehension

- Ask children to talk to their partner about the story. Have they ever had a race? Have they ever helped a friend who got into trouble? Take feedback.
- Ask children how Mim feels at different points in the story. Help children link Mim's feeling to their own. Have they ever felt scared, upset or relieved?
- Use **Mog and Mim: Resource sheet 2** to explore Mim's feelings further.

Extending vocabulary

- Ask children to talk about the actions the aliens do. Take feedback.
- Make a list of verbs: **dash**, **dart**, **speed**, **bounce**, **plod**, **sprint**, **lumber** and so on. Demonstrate each action, asking children to copy.
- Hold up two verbs, read them and ask: *Which is quicker?* Repeat until you have an ordered line according to speed.
- Make sentences together using the verbs, for example: *Mim trudged, but Mog dashed by.*

Reading for pleasure

Beegu Alexis Deacon
Man on the Moon Simon Bartram
Q Pootle 5 Nick Butterworth
Toys in Space Mini Grey

102 © HarperCollins*Publishers* 2018

Mog and Mim: Resource sheet 1
Phonic focus: /b/, /f/ and /ff/

Name: _____

Say the phoneme. Talk about the picture. Trace the grapheme.

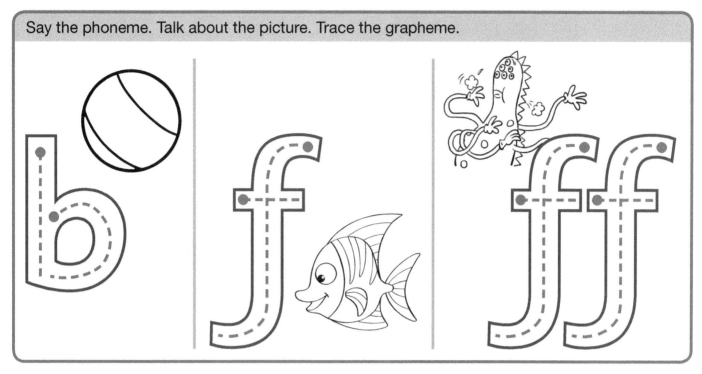

Read the words. What begins with /b/? Circle the correct pictures. Talk about the pictures.

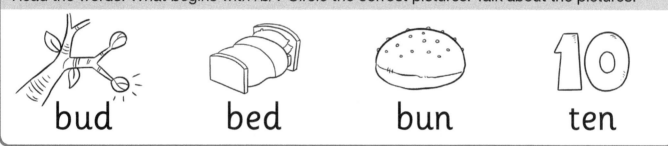

bud   bed   bun   ten

Read the words. What begins with /f/? Circle the correct pictures. Talk about the pictures.

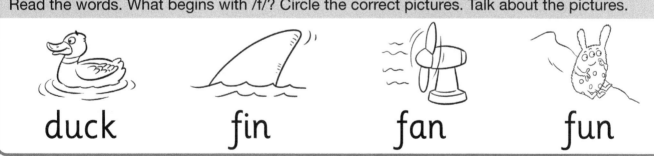

duck   fin   fan   fun

Read the words. What ends with /ff/? Circle the correct pictures. Talk about the pictures.

cuff   puff   rat   off

Mog and Mim: Resource sheet 2
Comprehension (Character) and Vocabulary

Name: _____

Talk about how Mim feels through the story.

What words could you use instead of tired? For example: sleepy, shattered, exhausted, drained, drowsy, jaded, worn out.

Bad Luck, Dad (Chant and Chatter Book 12)

Book band: Pink B

This is a non-fiction book about a fishing trip. Dad is keen to catch a cod. He has a big rod and all the equipment. Will he be lucky this time?

Practising phonics Phase 2

Warm up: Reading high frequency words
- Write these words on cards: **him**, **had**, **dog**, **off**, **back**, **but**, **big**, **of**, **off**, **will**.
- Ask children to help you put sound buttons on the words, and underline any digraphs.
- Ask children to read the words independently: put your finger underneath each sound so they know which letter to read.

  New: Practise the sounds /j/ /v/ /w/ /x/ /y/ /z/

  Focus: /l/ /ll/ /ss/

  Review: /s/ /a/ /t/ /p/ /i/ /n/ /m/ /d/ /g/ /o/ /c/ /k/ /ck/ /e/ /u/ /r/ /h/ /b/ /f/ /ff/

- Introduce the new sounds to prepare for reading Red A books (see page 69).
- Make sure children are confident reading these sounds.
- Use **Bad Luck, Dad: Resource sheet 1** to introduce the focus sounds. Show children the images of a leaf, a bell and a mess to help them link the grapheme to the phoneme. Ask children to say the sound as they trace the letter.
- Tell children to match the pictures to the focus sounds: /l/, /ll/ and /ss/.

Decoding practice
- Practise reading the words on the front page of the book.
- Ask children to complete the final activity on **Bad Luck, Dad: Resource sheet 1**. Tell them to read the words.

Children read
- Tell children to read the book aloud. Encourage them to sound out the words and explore the pictures.
- Listen to children as they read.
- When children have finished reading, ask them to find things on pages 14–15 that include the focus sounds /l/, /ll/ and /ss/.

After reading

Developing fluency
- Read each chant aloud and ask children to follow in their books.
  - Tell children to join in with you as you read.
  - Hesitate as you read so children can take over reading the next word.
- Tell children what you are thinking as you read so they can see how you make links between the words and the story, for example: *When I read 'Dad tugs the rod. No! Dad lets the cod go', I imagine Dad has a big fish on the end of his fishing line, and he is tugging at it. But when Dad pulls his rod up there is nothing on the end of his line. Poor Dad!*
- Read each chant with expression and ask children to have a go at reading with expression to a partner.
- Have fun with the chants, enjoy the rhythm and make up actions to bring them to life!

Comprehension
- Ask children to imagine they are going to catch a fish. Tell them to act out the actions as you narrate: *First, thread the bait onto your hook. Careful, it's sharp! Pull your rod back and cast your line. Now wait … Oh, a nibble, and another nibble. Now wind up your reel and pull. Tug hard! It's a gigantic cod! Oh no, it's escaped! Better luck next time.*

Extending vocabulary
Other words for big
- Say: *Dad thought he had caught a big fish! But that fish wasn't just big, it was huge!*
- Ask children to repeat: *It was a huge fish.*
- Say that **enormous** is even bigger than **huge**: *Dad thought he had caught a huge fish! But that fish wasn't just huge, it was enormous!*
- Ask children to repeat: *It was an enormous fish.*
- Repeat for the word **gigantic**.
- Ask children to use one of the new words to describe the fish to their partner.

Reading for pleasure

Bear & Hare Go Fishing Emily Gravett
One Smart Fish Christopher Wormell

Fishing with Grandma Susan Avingaq

Bad Luck, Dad: Resource sheet 1
Phonic focus: /l/, ll/ and /ss/

Name: _____

Say the phoneme. Talk about the picture. Trace the grapheme.

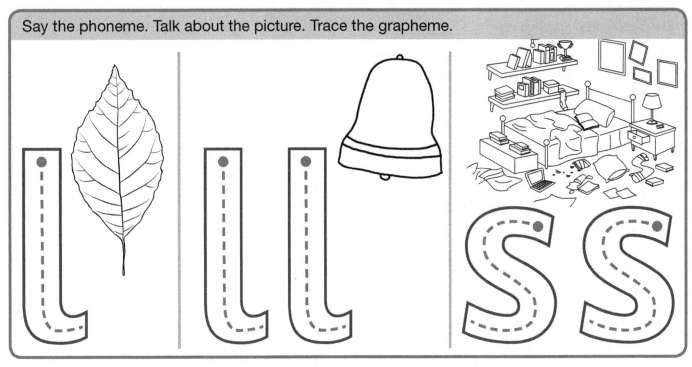

What begins with /l/? Circle the correct pictures.

Read the words. What ends with /ll/? Circle the correct pictures. Talk about the pictures.

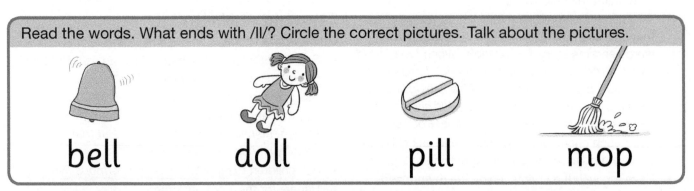

bell   doll   pill   mop

Read the words. What ends with /ss/? Circle the correct pictures. Talk about the pictures.

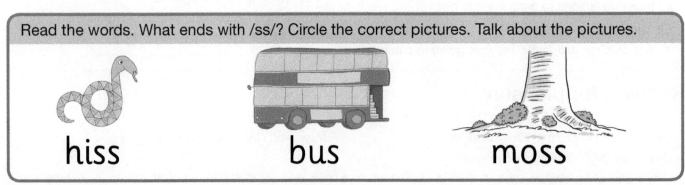

hiss   bus   moss

Bad Luck, Dad: Resource sheet 2
Comprehension (Sequencing) and Vocabulary

Name: _____

Talk about what happens when Dad gets the cod. Put the pictures in order.

Think about what happens next. Draw what happens next.

What words could you use to describe the size of the fish?

© HarperCollins*Publishers* 2018   Pink B: Bad Luck, Dad   107

Support for Red books
Introduction

John Sweller says we need to reduce strain on the working memory. The reasons for this are:
- The working memory has finite capacity.
- We can only process a small amount of new information at a time. Recent studies suggest this is only five (plus or minus two) new things at a time.
- We need to chunk knowledge together to make it manageable. This framework of information is called a 'schema'. A schema helps us build one big 'chunk' of knowledge.
- The schema for reading is phonics.
- Children need to build up and practise their phonic knowledge over time so that each chunk connects to the schema.

Practise the phonemes and graphemes children know. Incrementally add new graphemes.

Ensure you use the same formula when teaching, so children don't have to process a new way of learning as well as new information.

Source: John Sweller et al: 'Cognitive Load Theory: Advances in Research on Worked Example, Animations, and Cognitive Load Measurement' *Educational Psychology Review* December 2010, Volume 22

Reading multi-syllabic words

Children will read words with two or more syllables from Red A onwards. This is a great way of embedding phonic knowledge. Reading multi-syllabic words with ease is crucial to developing fluency.

*Teaching two-syllable words: **rocket***
- Bend the card so only the first syllable is showing: **rock**.
- Find the digraph. Dot and underline. Ask children to read: **rock**.
- Display the second syllable: **et**. Dot and underline as needed.
- Show children the whole word: **rocket**. Ask children to blend each part: **rock/et**. Say the word: *rocket*.
- Ensure children understand the meaning of the word.

Red A Link to Phase 3

	New	Review
Sounds	j, v, w, x, y, z, zz, qu ch, sh, th, ng, nk	a, e, i, o, u, p, b, d, ck, ff, ll, ss (These graphemes are from Pink (Chant and Chatter) books and will need extra practice.)
High frequency words	this, with, that, then, them, yes, will	an, as, it, in, am, at, dad, can, get, up, not, mum, him, had, dog, on, back, but, big, if, off, and
Common exception words	was, you, her, we, my, they, are, put, push	his, I, is, the, go, to, has, into

(See pages 22–23 *How to teach common exception words* for an example lesson plan.)

108 © HarperCollins*Publishers* 2018

Red B Link to Phase 3

	New	Review
Sounds	ai, ee, igh, oa, oo, *oo*, ar, or, ur, ow, oi, ear, air, ure, er + double letters	j, v, w, x, y, z, qu, zz, ch, sh, th, ng, nk (These graphemes are from Red A and will need extra practice.)
High frequency words	this, with, that, then, them, yes, for, now, down, see, look, too	an, as, it, in, am, at, dad, can, get, up, not, mum, him, had, dog, on, back, but, big, if, off, will, and
Common exception words	You will read these common exception words: my, they, are, we, you, put, by, pull, push	is, I, the, go, no

(See pages 22–23 *How to teach common exception words* for an example lesson plan.)

What to teach while reading Red books

What to teach while reading Red A

Children will be able to move on to the Red B reading books with Phase 3 graphemes when they are able to read graphemes in the box below and blend them into words with confidence.

> ai, ee, igh, oa, oo, *oo*, ar, or, ur, ow, oi, ear, air, ure, er

Use assessment to work out which Phase 3 graphemes from the Red A books children find tricky and review them regularly. Typically, they are:

> j, v, w, x, y, z, zz, qu, ch, sh, th, ng, nk

For each book use the:
- phonic warm up to reinforce oral blending skills
- phonic activities to practise reading graphemes and words
- phonic activity sheet to practise the focus grapheme for the book you are reading.

What to teach while reading Red B

Children will be able to move on to the Yellow reading books with Phase 4 graphemes when they are able to read adjacent consonants in words with a short vowel sound. There are some example words in the box below:

> end   act   stop   lunch   crack   splash   scrunch

Use assessment to work out which Phase 3 graphemes from the Red B books children find tricky and review them regularly. Typically, they are:

> ai, ee, igh, oa, oo, *oo*, ar, or, ur, ow, oi, ear, air, ure, er

© HarperCollins*Publishers* 2018

Support for Red books Introduction

Preparing for Yellow books

Teaching

- Continue to teach or review a sound every day. The focus at Phase 4 in the Yellow books is on blending adjacent consonants with short vowel sounds.
- Continue to teach word reading. Ensure children can recognise digraphs and trigraphs.

Assessment

- Assess all Reception children once they have been taught all the Phase 3 phonemes. Use the assessment on pages 26–34 to place children at the appropriate band.
- Use the subsequent assessments every six weeks to ensure speedy progress.

Reading for pleasure

- Read aloud to children every day.
- Consider reading the *Reading for pleasure* books to enhance the *Big Cat Phonics for Letters and Sounds* book children are reading.
- Make connections between the books you read aloud to children and the *Big Cat Phonics for Letters and Sounds* books, so children see themselves as readers.
- Explain any unusual words in these books to help children grow their vocabulary.
- Return to well-loved books. Repeated reading helps children internalise these stories, which helps their comprehension and writing.

Research

- For children, there is a clear link between reading frequency and reading enjoyment.
- Children who enjoy reading benefit emotionally and socially. Reading can increase empathy.
- Children who read widely often have better general knowledge.
- Stories at a level beyond children's current reading level increase their exposure to new and ambitious vocabulary. Talking about these words widens children's vocabularies.

Christina Clark and Kate Rumbold, 'Reading for Pleasure: A research overview', *National Literacy Trust*, 2006

This is My Kit

Book band: Red A

This non-fiction book shows you how to make a battery using a kit and a lemon.

Practising phonics Phase 3

Warm up: Two-syllable words
- Write these words on cards: **lemon, bucket, liquid.**
- Bend the card over to show one syllable: **buck**.
- Ask children to identify the digraphs and underline them. Ask them to read the sounds and blend.
- Repeat for the second syllable: **et**.
- Show the whole word. Ask children to read each syllable buck/et and then read the whole word: **bucket**.

Practise the sounds /th/ /nk/ /x/ /ch/ /ng/ /zz/

Review: /i/ /e/ /o/ /u/ /ck/ /b/ /p/ /ff/

- Introduce the new sounds to practise the Phase 3 sounds in this book.
- Make sure children are confident at reading these sounds.
- Use **This is My Kit: Resource sheet 1** to introduce the focus sounds. Show children the images of the chimp, the thorn and the ring to help them link the graphemes to the phonemes. Ask children to say the sounds as they trace the letters.
- Tell children to match the pictures to the focus sounds: **/ch/, /th/** and **/ng/**.

Decoding practice
- Practise reading the words on the front page of the book.
- Children complete the final activity on **This is My Kit: Resource sheet 1**. Tell them to read the words.

Children read
- Tell children to read the book aloud. Encourage them to sound out the words and explore the pictures.
- Listen to children as they read.
- When children have finished reading, ask them to find things on pages 14–15 that include the focus sounds **/ch/, /th/** and **/ng/**.

After reading

Developing fluency
- Read aloud and ask children to follow in their books.
  - Tell children to join in with you as you read.
  - Hesitate as you read so children can take over reading the next word.
- Tell children what you are thinking as you read so they can see how you make links between the words and the story, for example: *When I read the labels on pages 2 and 3, I can see that each label helps me know what is in the kit.* Ask children to read the labels and match them to the objects.
- Read the book with expression and ask children to have a go at reading with expression to a partner.

Comprehension
- Children talk about the book. Have they ever done a science experiment? Take feedback.
- Ask children to talk about why the lemon might be important. Do they think the buzzer will work without the lemon?
- Ask children to help you label all the items in the kit on **This is My Kit: Resource sheet 2**. Ask them to help you work out what each item does by looking back in the book.

Extending vocabulary
- Explain that instructions tell us how to do something. They start with a word that tells us what to do – a verb.
- Ask children to find the words that start each instruction: **pick, push, link, fix**.
- Give children simple instructions to move from one part of the playground to another. Vary the verbs you use so that they move in different ways.

Reading for pleasure

Crafting With Kids Catherine Woram
The Curious Kid's Science Book Asia Citro
Ada Twist, Scientist Andrea Beaty
Gravity Jason Chin

© HarperCollins*Publishers* 2018

This is My Kit: Resource sheet 1
Phonic focus: /ch/, /th/ and /ng/

Name: _____

Say the phoneme. Talk about the picture. Trace the grapheme.

What begins with /ch/? Circle the correct picture.

What begins with /th/? Circle the correct picture.

What ends with /ng/? Circle the correct picture.

Read the words.

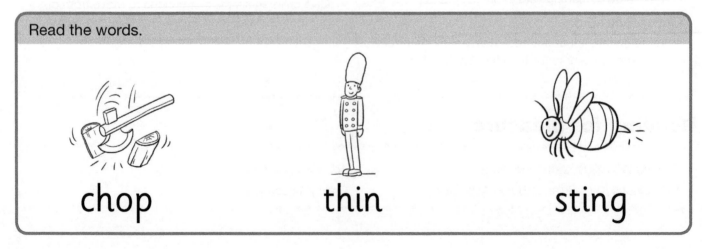

chop   thin   sting

This is My Kit: Resource sheet 2
Comprehension (Sequencing) and Vocabulary

Name: _____

Number or cut out the pictures to order them.

Label the kit from the book correctly. Talk about the kit.

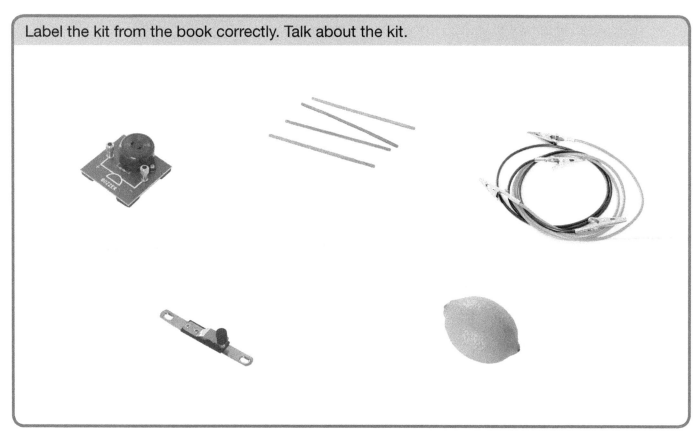

© HarperCollins*Publishers* 2018   Red A: This is My Kit   113

Zip and Zigzag

Book band: Red A

The Zigzag team love to skateboard, but who are their mysterious top skaters?

Practising phonics Phase 3

Warm up: Reading words with the digraphs: /qu/, /th/, /nk/, /ck/, /ss/

- Write these words on cards: **think**, **quick**, **mess**, **then**. Show children a card: **think**.
- Ask children to look for digraphs in the word (two letters that make one sound).
- Draw a dot beneath each single letter that makes a sound /i/, and a line beneath each digraph /th/ and /nk/. Remind children that the line shows two letters are making one sound.
- Ask children to read each sound and blend the word: **th/i/nk**. Repeat for the other words.

  Practise the sounds /qu/ /j/ /v/ /z/ /th/ /nk/

  Review: /a/ /o/ /e/ /i/ /u/ /p/ /d/ /b/ /ck/ /ss/ /ff/ /ll/ /k/

- Introduce the new sounds to practise the Phase 3 sounds in this book.
- Make sure children are confident at reading these sounds.
- Use **Zip and Zigzag: Resource sheet 1** to introduce the focus sound. Show children the images of the jelly and vulture to help them link the graphemes to the phonemes. Ask children to say the sounds as they trace the letters.
- Tell children to match the pictures to the focus sounds: /j/ and /v/.

Decoding practice

- Practise reading the words on the front page of the book.
- Children complete the final activity on **Zip and Zigzag: Resource sheet 1**. Tell them to read the words.

Children read

- Tell children to read the book aloud. Encourage them to sound out the words and explore the pictures.
- Listen to children as they read.
- When children have finished reading, ask them to find things on pages 14–15 that include the focus sounds /j/ and /v/.

After reading

Developing fluency

- Read the book aloud and ask children to follow in their books.
  - Tell children to join in with you as you read.
  - Hesitate as you read so children can take over reading the next word.
- Tell children what you are thinking as you read so they can see how you make links between the words and the story, for example: *When I read the sentence on pages 2 and 3, I can see children getting ready to go off on a skateboarding adventure. I am excited about what they might do.*
- Read the book with expression and ask children to have a go at reading with expression to a partner.

Comprehension

- Children to talk to their partner about the story. Do they go to the park? What do they do there?
- Show children the story map on **Zip and Zigzag: Resource sheet 2**. Retell the story together.
- Ask children to use the story map to help them retell the story to their partner. They can add words or labels to the map if they wish.

Extending vocabulary

Verbs

- Talk about the movements the children in the story made on their skateboards: **rocketed**, **zigzagged** and **jetted**.
- Make a list of more verbs to describe the skateboarders' movements: **zoomed**, **raced**, **darted**, **shot**, **whooshed** and so on. Help children understand what each movement looks like by demonstrating. Get children to zoom or whoosh and so on.
- Create a line-up of speed with children. Hold up two words, read them, and ask: *Which is quicker?* Continue to compare words until all the words have been put in order.
- Help children to compose sentences that use the words in context, for example: *Jess darted and Vic shot by.*

Reading for pleasure

Shark in the Park! Nick Sharratt

Percy's Bumpy Ride Nick Butterworth

The Park in the Dark Martin Waddell

You Choose Nick Sharratt and Pippa Goodhart

Zip and Zigzag: Resource sheet 1
Phonic focus: /j/ and /v/

Name: _____

Say the phoneme. Talk about the picture. Trace the grapheme.

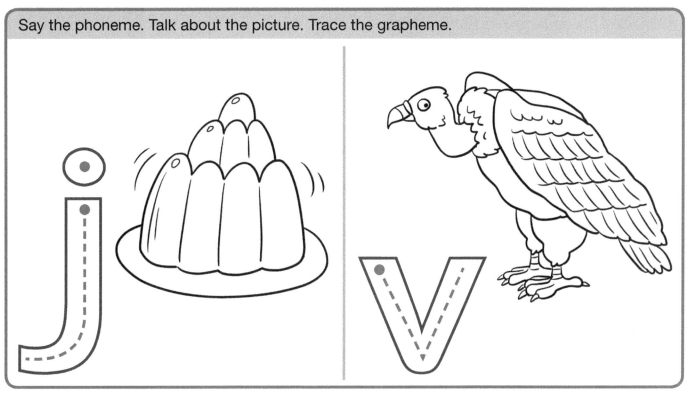

What begins with /j/? Circle the correct picture.

What begins with /v/? Circle the correct picture.

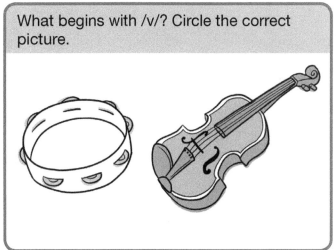

Read the words.

jam   van   jet

© HarperCollins*Publishers* 2018   Red A: Zip and Zigzag   115

Zip and Zigzag: Resource sheet 2
Comprehension (Recalling) and Vocabulary

Name: _____

Remember the story and order the pictures.

Which words mean fast? For example: quick, speedy, hasty, dash, rapid, swift, like lightning, zip, whoosh, whiz, rocket, jet, zoom. Discuss which of these words you would use to describe each image below.

116   Red A: Zip and Zigzag

Big Mud Run

Book band: Red A

This is a non-fiction book about a muddy fun run for children. It explores the obstacles and activities children would have to surmount on a run.

Practising phonics Phase 3

Warm up: Reading high frequency words
- Write these words on cards: **this**, **with**, **that**, **then**, **them**, **yes**, **will**.
- Ask children to help you put sound buttons and dashes on the words, one button/dash under each sound.
- Ask children to read the words independently. Put your finger underneath each sound so they know which letter(s) to read.

Practise the sounds /sh/ /nk/ /ng/ /th/ /w/ /qu/ /z/ /j/

Review: /ff/ /d/ /u/ /a/ /o/ /ck/ /i/ /b/ /ll/

- Introduce the new sounds to practise the Phase 3 sounds in this book.
- Make sure children are confident at reading these sounds.
- Use **Big Mud Run: Resource sheet 1** to introduce the focus sounds. Show children the images of the window and the quilt to help them link the graphemes to the phonemes. Ask children to say each sound as they trace the letter.
- Tell children to match the pictures to the focus sounds: **/w/** and **/qu/**.

Decoding practice
- Practise reading the words on the front page of the book.
- Children complete the final activity on **Big Mud Run: Resource sheet 1**. Tell them to read the words.

Children read
- Tell children to read the book aloud. Encourage them to sound out the words and explore the pictures.
- Listen to children as they read.
- When children have finished reading, ask them to find things on pages 14–15 that include the focus sounds **/w/** and **/qu/**.

After reading

Developing fluency
- Read the book aloud and ask children to follow in their books.
  - Tell children to join in with you as you read.
  - Hesitate as you read so children can take over reading the next word.
- Tell children what you are thinking as you read so they can see how you make links between the words and the information, for example: *When I read the question 'Can you go on a mud run?', I can tell it's a question because of the word 'can' at the beginning and the question mark at the end. I know this question is introducing me to the main idea of this book – going on a mud run.*
- Read the book with expression and ask children to have a go at reading with expression to a partner.

Comprehension
- Ask children to talk to their partner about the mud run. Do they play outdoors and get muddy? Have they ever been on a run – a park run, for example?
- Explain that non-fiction books have different features from story books. This book has labels that give extra information. Ask children to read the labels on each page.
- Compose some labels for the map of the Big Mud Run on **Big Mud Run: Resource sheet 2**.

Extending vocabulary
Onomatopoeia
- Tell children that some words help us hear sounds. For example, the word **squelch** sounds a lot like the sound of landing in sticky mud!
- Look at the activities in the book and discuss the sounds you might hear: **splash**, **groan**, **huff**, **puff**, **grunt**, **ooze**, **splat**, **squish**, **thud** and so on.
- Make sound effects for each picture to bring it alive.

Reading for pleasure

The Wild Weather Book: Loads of things to do outdoors in rain, wind and snow Fiona Danks and Jo Schofield

Ready Steady Mo! Mo Farah

Dinosaur Chase! Benedict Blathwayt

Mud Mary Lyn Ray

© HarperCollins*Publishers* 2018

Big Mud Run: Resource sheet 1
Phonic focus: /w/ and /qu/

Name: _____

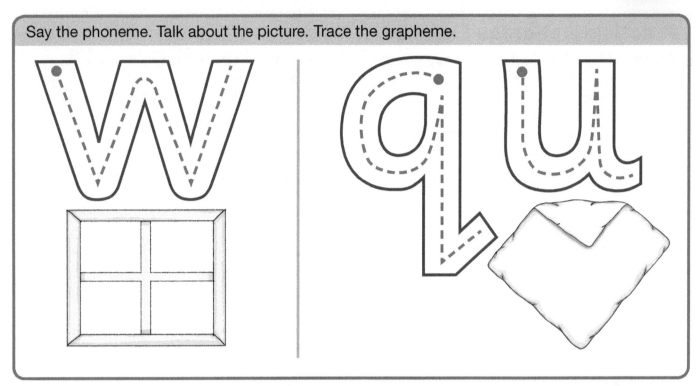

Say the phoneme. Talk about the picture. Trace the grapheme.

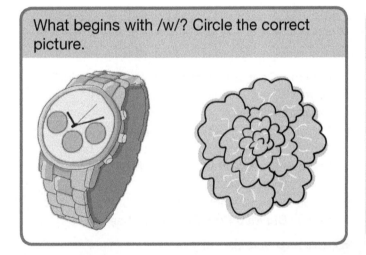

What begins with /w/? Circle the correct picture.

What begins with /qu/? Circle the correct picture.

Read the words.

wig   quack   quick

Red A: Big Mud Run

Big Mud Run: Resource sheet 2
Comprehension (Recalling) and Vocabulary

Name: _____

Can you recall the mud run and label the map below?

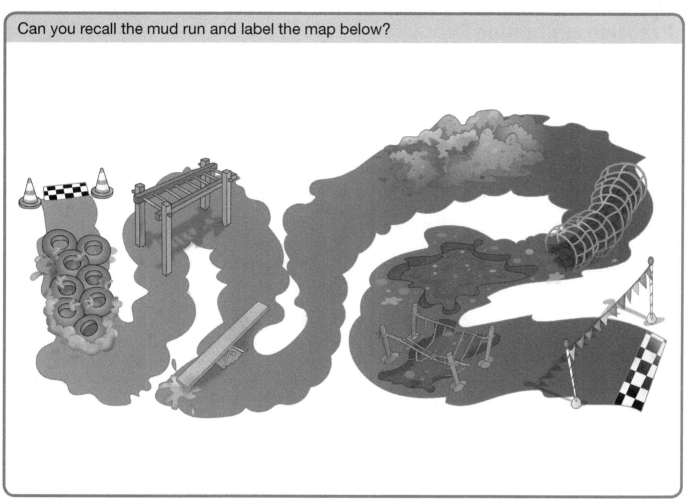

What sound words can you use to describe sounds in the picture? For example: squelch, splash, splosh, whistle, screech, quack, woof, whiz, cheer, ringing, bleeping, huffing, puffing, wailing, tweeting, clicking. Talk about the picture.

Fantastic Yak

Book band: Red A

This is a story about a yak who feels sad. But soon he realises that helping others makes him feel good!

Practising phonics Phase 3

Warm up: Sound buttons and digraphs

- Write these words on cards: **yes**, **chop**, **box**, **that**, **wet**, **chink**.
- Show children a card: **that**.
- Ask children to look for the digraphs in the word (two letters that make one sound).
- Draw a dot beneath each sound and a line beneath the digraph **/th/**. Remind children that this shows two letters are making one sound.
- Ask children to read each sound and blend the word.
- Repeat for the other words.

> Practise the sounds /y/ /x/ /ch/ /th/ /nk/

> Review: /ck/ /d/ /p/ /e/ /o/ /a/ /e/ /u/ /f/

- Introduce the new sounds to practise the Phase 3 sounds in this book.
- Make sure children are confident at reading these sounds.

- Use **Fantastic Yak: Resource sheet 1** to introduce the focus sounds. Show children the images of a yoghurt and a fox to help them link the grapheme to the phoneme. Ask children to say the sounds as they trace the letters.
- Tell children to match the pictures to the focus sounds: **/y/** and **/x/**.

Decoding practice

- Practise reading the words on the front page of the book.
- Children complete the final activity on **Fantastic Yak: Resource sheet 1**. Tell them to read the words.

Children read

- Tell children to read the book aloud. Encourage them to sound out the words and explore the pictures.
- Listen to children as they read.
- When children have finished reading, ask them to find things on pages 14–15 that include the focus sounds **/y/** and **/x/**.

After reading

Developing fluency

- Read the book aloud and ask children to follow in their books.
  - Tell children to join in with you as you read.
  - Hesitate as you read so children can take over reading the next word.
- Tell children what you are thinking as you read so they can see how you make links between the words and the story, for example: *When Yak says 'I am fed up' I know he is sad. So I can say it with a sad voice to show how Yak is feeling.* Ask children to read Yak's speech in a sad voice.
- Read the book with expression and ask children to have a go at reading with expression to a partner.

Comprehension

- Ask children to talk to their partner about the good deeds Yak did. Have they ever helped someone? What did it feel like? Take feedback.
- Talk about how Yak fixed the socks and the pot. Narrate the actions Yak might have done: *Yak took out the wool. He got out his knitting needles and then be began to knit.*
- Ask children to act out Yak handing his gifts to Fox and Chicken. How do they think each character feels? Use **Fantastic Yak: Resource sheet 2** to write the characters' feelings in the thought bubbles.

Extending vocabulary

Synonyms

- Read the title of the book: *Fantastic Yak*. Ask children to talk to their partner about why Yak was fantastic. Take feedback.
- Tell children there are other words they could use to describe Yak: **marvellous**, **amazing**, **wonderful**, **terrific**, **fabulous**.
- Practise saying a short sentence using the new words with children: *Yak was kind. He was _____! Yak was helpful. He was _____!*
- Ask children which word they think describes Yak best and why.

Reading for pleasure

Farmer Duck Martin Waddell

The Rainbow Fish Marcus Pfister

Pumpkin Soup Helen Cooper

Fantastic Yak: Resource sheet 1
Phonic focus: /y/ and /x/

Name: _____

Say the phoneme. Talk about the picture. Trace the grapheme.

What begins with /y/? Circle the correct picture.

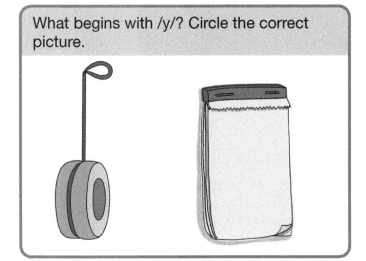

What ends with /x/? Circle the correct picture.

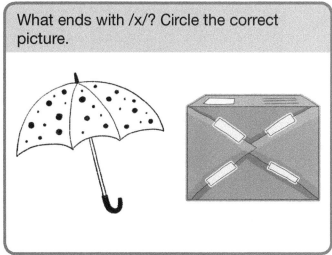

Read the words.

wax　　　　　yak　　　　　six

© HarperCollins*Publishers* 2018　　　　　Red A: Fantastic Yak　　121

Fantastic Yak: Resource sheet 2
Comprehension (Character) and Vocabulary

Name: _____

Write or draw in the thought bubbles to show how each character feels.

Describe how Yak feels in the story. What words can you think of that mean sad? For example: upset, miserable, depressed, low, grumpy, unhappy, distressed, inconsolable, distraught.

In the Fish Tank

Book band: Red A

This is a non-fiction book about setting up a fish tank. Jez and his dad show us how it is done.

Practising phonics Phase 3

Warm up: What's in the box?

- Hide some objects or pictures in a box: shell, fish, pink, ring, zip, box.
- Tell children they must work out what is in the box.
- Display the letters of the word in order, for example: **sh-e-ll**. Ask children to read the letters and blend them.
- Ask children to shout out the answer to: *What's in the box?*
- Show children the object or picture.
- Repeat for other objects.

> Practise the sounds /nk/ /sh/ /z/ /j/ /y/ /x/
>
> Review: /ck/ /a/ /e/ /i/ /o/ /u/ /ll/ /p/ /d/

- Introduce the new sounds to practise the Phase 3 sounds in this book.
- Make sure children are confident at reading these sounds.
- Use **In the Fish Tank: Resource sheet 1** to introduce the focus sounds. Show children the images of the shell and the drink to help them link the graphemes to the phonemes. Ask children to say the sounds as they trace the letters.
- Tell children to match the pictures to the focus sounds: **/sh/** and **/nk/**.

Decoding practice

- Practise reading the words on the front page of the book.
- Ask children to complete the final activity on **In the Fish Tank: Resource sheet 1**. Tell them to read the words.

Children read

- Tell children to read the book aloud. Encourage them to sound out the words and explore the pictures.
- Listen to children as they read.
- When children have finished reading, ask them to find things on pages 14–15 that include the focus sounds **/sh/** and **/nk/**.

After reading

Developing fluency

- Read the book aloud and ask children to follow in their books.
  - Tell children to join in with you as you read.
  - Hesitate as you read so children can take over reading the next word.
- Tell children what you are thinking as you read so they can see how you make links between the words and the information, for example: *I can see that Jez is choosing which things to put in his tank. His Dad is telling him what to do. When I see the word 'my' I know this is Jez talking about himself.*
- Read the book with expression and ask children to have a go at reading with expression to a partner.

Comprehension

- Ask children to talk to their partner about the book. Do they have pets at home? Have they ever looked after a pet? What did they need to do?
- Tell children that this book has instructions in it to help someone set up a fish tank. Explain that instructions start with the word that tells you what to do: a verb.
- Read the instructions on **In the Fish Tank: Resource sheet 2** together. Underline the verbs that start each instruction.
- Ask children to act out setting up the tank using the instructions.

Extending vocabulary

Sequencing

- Look through the book with children and model using sequencing words and phrases to signpost the order of events. For example: ***First*** *Jez and his Dad unpacked the tank,* ***next*** *they put some rocks inside the tank* and so on.
- Work together to use **first**, **next**, **after that** and **finally** as you retell the instructions together.
- Ask children to take turns at retelling the instructions using the sequencing words.

Reading for pleasure

Charlie & Lola: We Honestly Can Look After Your Dog Lauren Child

The Pet Person Jeanne Willis and Tony Ross

How to Look After Your Goldfish David Alderton

The New Puppy Catherine and Laurence Anholt

© HarperCollins*Publishers* 2018

In the Fish Tank: Resource sheet 1
Phonic focus: /sh/ and /nk/

Name: _____

Say the phoneme. Talk about the picture. Trace the grapheme.

What begins with /sh/? Circle the correct picture.

What ends with /nk/? Circle the correct picture.

Read the words.

shed   ink   fish tank

In the Fish Tank: Resource sheet 2
Comprehension (Sequencing) and Vocabulary

Name: _____

Read the instructions. Match the instructions to the pictures.

| Pop a ship in the tank. | Put a shell in the tank. | Put pink rocks in the tank. |

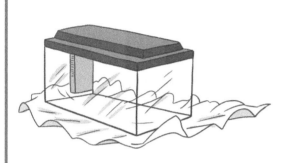  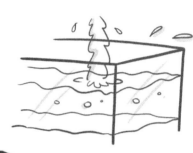

Get the tank.   Fill up the tank.

Draw the fish you would have in your fish tank. Can you describe them? What words can you think of to describe how fish move? For example: swim, dart, dive, bob, dash, wriggle.

Up in a Rocket

Book band: Red A

This is book is about a boy with a magic rocket that takes him up to space for an adventure.

Practising phonics Phase 3

Warm up: Alien words

- Practise the graphemes children know by reading alien words.
- Write each of these words on a card and decorate it with an alien: **quib**, **fong**, **lish**, **pech**, **wix**.
- Tell children these words are the names of aliens. They are not real words.
- Show children a word: **quib**.
- Ask them to call out any digraphs: **/qu/**. Put one button under each sound and a dash under each digraph.
- Ask children to sound out and blend the word.
- **Tip:** Do not encourage children to read the word without blending. Do not spell alien words.

  Practise the sounds /w/ /z/ /ng/ /sh/ /zz/

  Review: /a/ /e/ /i/ /o/ /u/ /p/ /b/ /d/ /ck/ /ff/

- Introduce the new sounds to practise the Phase 3 sounds in this book.
- Make sure children are confident at reading these sounds.

- Use **Up in a Rocket: Resource sheet 1** to introduce the focus sounds. Show children the images of the zebra, the buzzy bees and the ring to help them link the graphemes to the phonemes. Ask children to say the sounds as they trace the letters.
- Tell children to match the pictures to the focus sounds: **/z/**, **/zz/** and **/ng/**.

Decoding practice

- Practise reading the words on the front page of the book.
- Ask children to complete the final activity on **Up in a Rocket: Resource sheet 1**. Tell them to read the words.

Children read

- Tell children to read the book aloud. Encourage them to sound out the words and explore the pictures.
- Listen to children as they read.
- When children have finished reading, ask them to find things on pages 14–15 that include the focus sounds **/z/**, **/zz/** and **/ng/**.

After reading

Developing fluency

- Read the book aloud and ask children to follow in their books.
  - Tell children to join in with you as you read.
  - Hesitate as you read so children can take over reading the next word.
- Tell children what you are thinking as you read so they can see how you make links between the words and the story, for example: *When I read 'My rocket shot up and off', I can see the rocket blast up out of the bedroom and into space. I think this is the beginning of a magical adventure.*
- Read the book with expression and ask children to have a go at reading with expression to a partner.

Comprehension

- Ask children to talk to their partner about the child's adventure. Have they read books or seen films set in space? Take feedback.
- Talk about the sequence of events in the story. Make

sure children understand how the rocket allows the child to have an adventure. What do children think happens to the rocket at the end of the adventure?
- When you are sure children are confident about the main events in the story ask them to use **Up in a Rocket: Resource sheet 2** to sequence the story.

Extending vocabulary

Comparisons

- Draw children's attention to pages 4–5 where the rocket gets bigger. Read 'big, big, big!' together.
- Tell children that the words **big**, **bigger** and **biggest** are linked. We use them to describe the size of one thing compared to another.
- Show children three objects and put them in size order together. Use **big**, **bigger** and **biggest** to describe them, for example: *This box is big, but this box is bigger, and this box is the biggest!*
- Repeat with the words **small**, **smaller** and **smallest** and **loud**, **louder** and **loudest**.

Reading for pleasure

The Way Back Home Oliver Jeffers

Bob and the Moon Tree Mystery Simon Bartram

Laika the Astronaut Owen Davey

© HarperCollins*Publishers* 2018

Up in a Rocket: Resource sheet 1
Phonic focus: /z/, /zz/ and /ng/

Name: _____

Say the phoneme. Talk about the picture. Trace the grapheme.

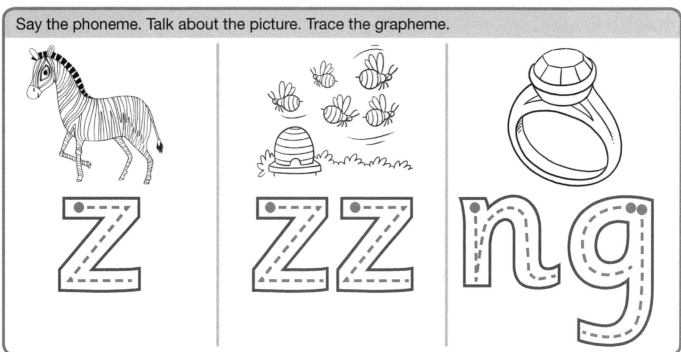

Read the words. What begins with /z/? Circle the correct pictures. Talk about the pictures.

zip　　　　　　　　cat　　　　　　　　zig zag

Read the words. What ends with /zz/? Circle the correct pictures. Talk about the pictures.

fizz　　　　　　　　buzz　　　　　　　　kiss

Read the words. What ends with /ng/? Circle the correct pictures. Talk about the pictures.

bank　　　　　　　　hang　　　　　　　　sing

© HarperCollins*Publishers* 2018　　　　　　　　Red A: Up in a Rocket

Up in a Rocket: Resource sheet 2
Comprehension (Sequencing) and Vocabulary

Name: _____

Look at the pictures. Number the scenes to put them in the correct order.

How is the child feeling in each picture? For example: surprised, asleep, happy. Talk about what you would do if you rocketed to space.

Red A: Up in a Rocket © HarperCollins*Publishers* 2018

Pink Boat, Pink Car

Book band: Red B

This is a story about how playing together and sharing toys can be tricky.

Practising phonics Phase 3

Warm up: High frequency words
- Write these words on cards: **for**, **now**, **down**, **see**, **look**, **too**.
- Ask children to help you put sound buttons on the words, one button under each sound and a dash under each digraph.
- Ask children to read the words independently. Put your finger underneath each sound so they know which letter(s) to read.

> **Practise the sounds /ar/ /oa/ /oo/ /oo/ /ure/ /ur/ /oi/ /air/**

> **Review: /nk/ /th/**

- Introduce the new sounds to practise the Phase 3 sounds in this book.
- Make sure children are confident reading these sounds.
- Use **Pink Boat, Pink Car: Resource sheet 1** to introduce the focus sounds: **/ure/** and **/oo/**.

Encourage children to read the phrase aloud to help them remember the sound each grapheme makes and then say the sound as they trace the letters.

Decoding practice
- Practise reading the words on the front page of the book.
- Ask children to complete the final activity on **Pink Boat, Pink Car: Resource sheet 1**. Tell them to read each word, then dot and dash it, and finally match it to the correct picture.

Children read
- Tell children to read the book aloud. Encourage them to sound out the words and explore the pictures.
- Listen to children as they read.
- When children have finished reading, ask them to talk with their partner to complete the activity on pages 14–15.

After reading

Developing fluency
- Read the book aloud and ask children to follow in their books.
  - Tell children to join in with you as you read.
  - Hesitate as you read so children can take over reading the next word.
- Tell children what you are thinking as you read so they can see how you make links between the words and the story, for example: *When I read Ella saying 'It is not fair!', I know she is a bit jealous of the boys and their toys. I think I might say 'not' more strongly to show how she is feeling.* Ask children to say the dialogue with feeling.
- Read the book with expression and ask children to have a go at reading with expression to a partner.

Comprehension
- Ask children to talk to their partner about the children in the book sharing the toys. Have they ever felt left out or jealous of someone? What did it feel like? Take feedback.
- Talk about the main action of the story. Check children understand the main events.
- Ask children to act out three parts of the story: Ella watching the boys with toys; Ella taking the toys; Ella asking the boys to play with her. How do they think each character feels? Use **Pink Boat, Pink Car: Resource sheet 2** to write the characters' feelings in the thought bubbles.

Extending vocabulary
- Read the sentence from page 10: *Ella did not feel good.* Ask children to recall why Ella might not feel good. Take feedback.
- Together make a list of words to describe Ella's feelings. Include some more challenging words such as: **dismayed**, **rotten**, **mean**. Make sure children understand the meaning of these words.
- Ask children to show you what the different emotions look like with their faces and bodies. Say: *Show me mean. Show me upset. Show me feeling rotten* and so on.

Reading for pleasure

It Was You, Blue Kangaroo! Emma Chichester Clark
I Want My Hat Back Jon Klassen
Oh No, George! Chris Haughton

© HarperCollins*Publishers* 2018

Pink Boat, Pink Car: Resource sheet 1
Phonic focus: /ure/ and /oo/

Name: _____

Mark the sound buttons. Find the digraphs in the words and underline them.

/ure/ a sure cure   /oo/ a cool pool

Match the words to the pictures.

moon   boot   rooftop   food

Read the words.

pure

manure

sure

cure   secure

Pink Boat, Pink Car: Resource sheet 2
Comprehension and Vocabulary

Name: _____

What are the children thinking in each picture? Write their thoughts in the thought bubbles.

Describe Ella's feelings, for example unhappy, upset, dismayed, rotten, mean.

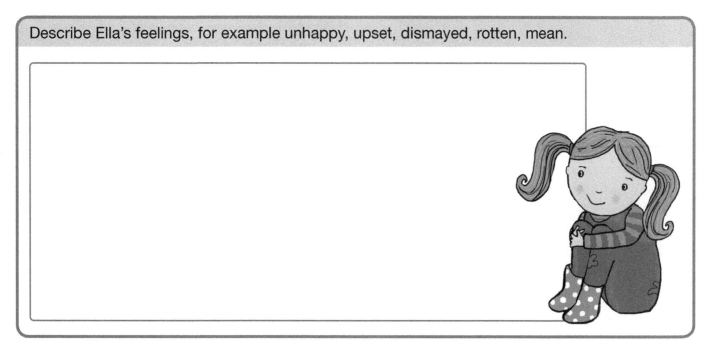

A Bee on a Lark

Book band: Red B

This is a rhyming story about the crazy antics of a bee and a bug.

Practising phonics Phase 3

Warm up: Rhyming words

- Write these words on cards: **park**, **mark**, **coat**, **goat**, **feel**, **peel**.
- Ask children to identify the digraphs. Underline them.
- Ask children to read each word. Tell them when words have the same end sound we say that they rhyme.
- Ask children to help you match the rhyming words. Read the rhyming words in pairs, asking children to listen for the rhyme.

> **Practise the sounds /ee/ /ar/ /oa/ /er/ /oo/, tt**

> **Review: /sh/ /th/ /x/ /j/**

- Introduce the new sounds to practise the Phase 3 sounds in this book.
- Use **Resource sheet 1** to introduce the focus sounds: **/ee/**, **/ar/** and **/er/**. Encourage children to read the phrase aloud to help them remember the sound each grapheme makes and then say the sound as they trace the letters.

Decoding practice

- Practise reading the words on the front page of the book.
- Ask children to complete the final activity on **A Bee on a Lark: Resource sheet 1**. Tell them to read each word, then dot and dash it, and finally match it to the correct picture.

Children read

- Tell children to read the book aloud. Encourage them to sound out the words and explore the pictures.
- Listen to children as they read.
- When children have finished reading, ask them to talk with their partner to complete the activity on pages 14–15.

After reading

Developing fluency

- Read the book aloud and ask children to follow in their books.
  - Tell children to join in with you as you read.
  - Hesitate as you read so children can take over reading the next word.
- Tell children what you are thinking as you read so they can see how you make links between the words and the story, for example: *When I read 'Titter, totter', I know the tower of animals and objects is wobbling. I am going to say it so it sounds like the animals are in danger. I am going to say it with feeling.* Ask children to say 'Titter, totter' with feeling.
- Read the book with expression and ask children to have a go at reading with expression to a partner.

Comprehension

- Ask children to talk to their partner about the story. Can they remember all the animals and all the objects? Take feedback.
- Use **A Bee on a Lark: Resource sheet 2** to remember which animals and objects were in each tower. Ask children to sort the animals and objects into two towers.
- Work together to retell the story, sequencing each tower.
- Ask children to cut out the pictures on **A Bee on a Lark: Resource sheet 2** to make their own towers as they retell the story.

Extending vocabulary

- Look at one of the towers just before it starts to tumble. Ask: *How many animals are there? How many objects are there? Does it look safe? Would you like to be in the tower?*
- Say the sentences below, asking children to repeat them and to act out 'shaky', 'wobbling like a jelly' and 'trembling'.

  The tower is shaky. The tower is wobbling like a jelly. The tower is trembling.

- Ask children to use their favourite sentence to describe the tower. Tell children to use their favourite word or phrase to complete the sentence on **A Bee on a Lark: Resource sheet 2**.

Reading for pleasure

Fox in Socks Dr. Seuss

Giant Jelly Jaws and the Pirates Helen Baugh and Ben Mantle

Pass the Jam, Jim Kaye Umansky

A Squash and a Squeeze Julia Donaldson and Axel Scheffler

© HarperCollins*Publishers* 2018

A Bee on a Lark: Resource sheet 1
Phonic focus: /ee/, /ar/ and /er/

Name: _____

Mark the sound buttons. Find the digraphs in the words and underline them.

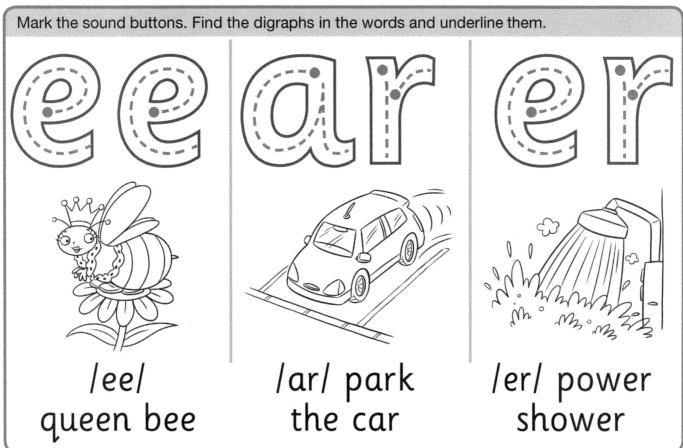

/ee/ queen bee   /ar/ park the car   /er/ power shower

Match the words to the pictures.

sheep   shark   tower   cart

beep   farmyard   shower   feet

© HarperCollins*Publishers* 2018   Red B: A Bee on a Lark

A Bee on a Lark: Resource sheet 2
Comprehension and Vocabulary

Name: _____

Cut out and sort the animals and objects and make the towers as you tell the story.

Write a word or sentence to describe the tower.

The tower is …

Wow Cow!

Book band: Red B

This book is an adventure story about a superhero cow called Wow Cow.

Practising phonics Phase 3

Warm up: Reading words with the digraphs: /oa/, /ow/, /ar/ and /ur/; and the trigraph /ear/

- Write these words on cards: **soap**, **town**, **hard**, **fur**, **near**.
- Show children a card: **soap**.
- Ask children to look for the digraph or trigraph in the word.
- Draw a dot beneath each sound and a line beneath the digraph **/oa/**. Remind children that this shows two letters are making one sound.
- Ask children to read each sound and blend the word. Ensure they understand what each word means.
- Repeat for the other words.

> **Practise the sounds** /oa/ /ee/ /oo/ /ar/ /ow/ /ear/ /oo/ /ur/ /n/, nn, /p/, pp

> **Review:** /sh/ /ch/ /w/

- Introduce the new sounds to practise the Phase 3 sounds in this book.
- Make sure children are confident reading these sounds.
- Use **Wow Cow!: Resource sheet 1** to introduce the focus sounds: **/ear/** and **/ow/**. Encourage children to read the phrase aloud to help them remember the sound each grapheme makes and then say the sound as they trace the letters.

Decoding practice

- Practise reading the words on the front page of the book.
- Ask children to complete the final activity on **Wow Cow!: Resource sheet 1**. Tell them to read each word, then dot and dash it, and finally match it to the correct picture.

Children read

- Tell children to read the book aloud. Encourage them to sound out the words and explore the pictures.
- Listen to children as they read.
- When children have finished reading, ask them to talk with their partner to complete the activity on pages 14–15.

After reading

Developing fluency

- Read the book aloud and ask children to follow in their books.
  - Tell children to join in with you as you read.
  - Hesitate as you read so children can take over reading the next word.
- Tell children what you are thinking as you read so they can see how you make links between the words and the story, for example: *When I read 'Wow Cow turns and turns', I can imagine Wow Cow spinning round using her amazing superhero powers. It is a very exciting part of the story!*
- Read the book with expression and ask children to have a go at reading with expression to a partner.

Comprehension

- Ask children to talk to their partner about how Wow Cow helped the goats. Take feedback.
- Use **Wow Cow!: Resource sheet 2** to identify the goats' problem and how Wow Cow solved it.

Extending vocabulary

- Ask children to read the word **fantastic** on page 11. Why do they think Wow Cow is fantastic? Take feedback.
- Tell children there are other words they could use to describe Wow Cow: **amazing**, **tremendous**, **extraordinary** and **excellent**.
- Practise saying a short sentence using the new words with children: *Wow Cow saved the day. She was _____! Wow Cow solved the mystery. She was _____!*
- Ask children which words they think describe Wow Cow best and why. Ask children to write the best words to describe Wow Cow on **Wow Cow!: Resource sheet 2**.

Reading for pleasure

Supertato Sue Hendra
Super Stan Matt Robertson

Zippo the Super Hippo Kes Gray

© HarperCollins*Publishers* 2018

Wow Cow!: Resource sheet 1
Phonic focus: /ear/ and /ow/

Name: _____

Mark the sound buttons. Find the digraphs or trigraphs in the words and underline them.

/ear/ my ears can hear

/ow/ How now, Wow Cow!

Match the words to the pictures.

ear   tear   fear   year

down   town   gown   cow

Wow Cow!: Resource sheet 2
Comprehension and Vocabulary

Name: _____

Discuss the goats' problem. Discuss how Wow Cow solves the problem. Write what the goats might say to Wow Cow and what Wow Cow might say to the goats.

Describe Wow Cow.

Wow Cow is …

Get Set For Fun

Book band: Red B

This is a non-fiction book about the exciting activities you can do when you are having fun outdoors.

Practising phonics Phase 3

Warm up: Reading two-syllable words

- Write these words on cards: **sunset**, **torchlight**, **ladder**, **rucksack**, **earwigs**.
- Bend the card over so it only shows one syllable: **torch**.
- Ask children to identify the digraphs (and trigraphs where appropriate) and underline them. Ask them to read the sounds and blend.
- Repeat for the second syllable: **light**.
- Show the whole word. Ask children to read each syllable **torch/light** and then read the whole word: **torchlight**.
- Ensure children understand the meaning of the word. Repeat for the other words.

> **Practise the sounds /oo/ /ar/ /ai/ /ow/ /oo/ /ear/ /ee/ /or/ /igh/ /er/, dd**

> **Review: /sh/ /ch/ /w/**

- Introduce the new sounds to practise the Phase 3 sounds in this book.

- Make sure children are confident reading these sounds.
- Use **Get Set For Fun: Resource sheet 1** to introduce the focus sounds: **/igh/** and **/or/**. Encourage children to read the phrase aloud to help them remember the sound each grapheme makes and then say the sound as they trace the letters.

Decoding practice

- Practise reading the words on the front page of the book.
- Ask children to complete the final activity on **Get Set For Fun: Resource sheet 1**. Tell them to read each word, then dot and dash it, and finally match it to the correct picture.

Children read

- Tell children to read the book aloud. Encourage them to sound out the words and explore the pictures.
- Listen to children as they read.
- When children have finished reading, ask them to talk with their partner to complete the activity on pages 14–15.

After reading

Developing fluency

- Read the book aloud and ask children to follow in their books.
  - Tell children to join in with you as you read.
  - Hesitate as you read so children can take over reading the next word.
- Tell children what you are thinking as you read so they can see how you make links between the words and the story, for example: *When I read 'Hear owls hoot in the dark', I imagine I am out at night listening to sounds of night animals.*
- Read the book with expression and ask children to have a go at reading with expression to a partner.

Comprehension

- Ask children to talk to their partner about having adventures outdoors. Have they ever made a den or rolled down a hill? Take feedback.

- Use the map on **Get Set For Fun: Resource sheet 2** to locate all the activities explored in the book. Make sure children can link the main places in the book to the map.
- Ask children to label the activities on the map, using the words in the word bank to help them.

Extending vocabulary

Verbs

- Help children make a list of verbs linked to the activities in the book: **climb**, **roll**, **skid**, **march**, **pelt**, **discover**, **search** and so on.
- Help children understand what each word looks like by demonstrating or using a contextualising sentence. Play 'Simon says' with the words.
- Ask children to draw a picture and describe their favourite outdoor activity on **Get Set For Fun: Resource sheet 2**. Challenge them to use accurate verbs.

Reading for pleasure

The Den Book Jo Schofield and Fiona Danks

Woodland Adventure Handbook Adam Dove

The Wild Woods Simon James

Stanley's Stick John Hegley

138

© HarperCollins*Publishers* 2018

Get Set For Fun: Resource sheet 1
Phonic focus: /igh/ and /or/

Name: _____

Mark the sound buttons. Find the digraphs and trigraphs in the words and underline them.

/igh/ night light   /or/ torn shorts

Match the words to the pictures.

Get Set For Fun: Resource sheet 2
Comprehension and Vocabulary

Name: _____

Talk about where you could do the activities from the book. Add labels to the map.

hill   ladder   rock   pool   den

Draw a picture of your favourite outdoor activity. Write words to describe the activities you can do outdoors.

It is Hidden

Book band: Red B

This is a non-fiction book that explores the amazing ways animals camouflage themselves.

Practising phonics Phase 3

Warm up: Double letters
- Write these words on cards: **button**, **hidden**, **sudden**, **puppet**.
- Show children a card: **button**.
- Tell children that the double letters **tt** make one sound: **/t/**.
- Draw a dot beneath each sound and a line beneath the double letters **tt**. Remind children that this shows two letters are making one sound.
- Ask children to read each sound and blend the word. Ensure they understand what the word means.
- Repeat for the other words.

> Practise the sounds /ee/ /oo/ /or/ /oa/ /ar/ /igh/ /oo/ /er/ /ow/, dd, tt

> Review: /th/ /sh/

- Introduce the new sounds to practise the Phase 3 sounds in this book.
- Use **It is Hidden: Resource sheet 1** to introduce the focus sounds: **/oo/** and **/ai/**. Encourage children to read the phrase aloud to help them remember the sound each grapheme makes and then say the sound as they trace the letters.

Decoding practice
- Practise reading the words on the front page of the book.
- Ask children to complete the final activity on **It is Hidden: Resource sheet 1**. Tell them to read each word, then dot and dash it, and finally match it to the correct picture.

Children read
- Tell children to read the book aloud. Encourage them to sound out the words and explore the pictures.
- Listen to children as they read.
- When children have finished reading, ask them to talk with their partner to complete the activity on pages 14–15.

After reading

Developing fluency
- Read the book aloud and ask children to follow in their books.
  - Tell children to join in with you as you read.
  - Hesitate as you read so children can take over reading the next word.
- Tell children what you are thinking as you read so they can see how you make links, for example: *When I read 'The toad is hidden at the bottom', the word 'bottom' tells me where to look on the page to find the toad.*
- Read the book with expression and ask children to have a go at reading with expression to a partner.

Comprehension
- Ask children to talk to their partner about how they found each animal in the book. What clues did they look for? Take feedback.
- Talk about the words that describe where you need to look on the page to find each animal. Direct children to words that give more information about where things are, such as: **at**, **on**, **by** and so on.
- Use these prepositions to describe where objects are in the classroom: *The light switch is by the door.*
- Ask children to use the prepositions on **It is Hidden: Resource sheet 2** to describe where the objects are.

Extending vocabulary
- Tell children that the word **camouflaged** means hidden by looking like your surroundings. Ask children to look at the hidden animals and talk about how they are camouflaged. Take feedback.
- Help children use the word **camouflage** in context: *The toad is camouflaged to look like a leaf. It is the same colour as the forest floor. It is hard to see.*
- Ask children to look at the camouflaged animal on **It is Hidden: Resource sheet 2** and describe to their partner how it is camouflaged. Tell them to write some words to label how the animal is hidden.

Reading for pleasure

Neon Leon Jane Clarke
The Mixed-Up Chameleon Eric Carle

Secrets of Animal Camouflage Carron Brown and Wesley Robins

It is Hidden: Resource sheet 1
Phonic focus: /oo/ and /ai/

Name: _____

Mark the sound buttons. Find the digraphs and trigraphs in the words and underline them.

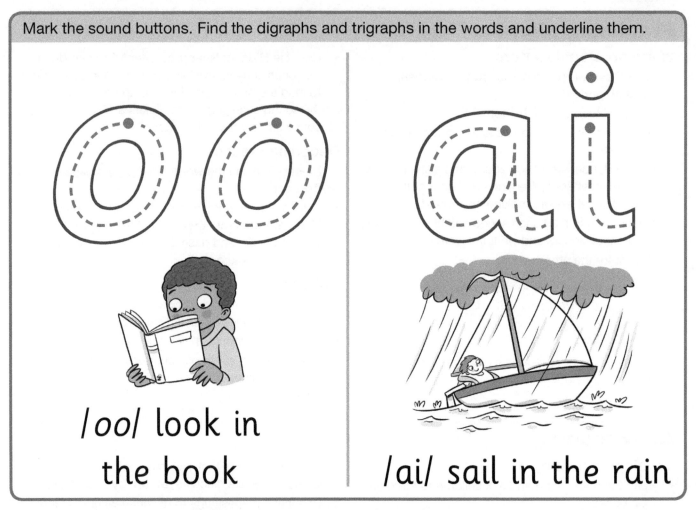

/oo/ look in the book

/ai/ sail in the rain

Match the words to the pictures.

nail   cook   tail   hood

shook   bait   hook   mail

It is Hidden: Resource sheet 2
Comprehension and Vocabulary

Name: _____

Look at the picture. Choose a preposition from the word bank to describe where the animal or person is.

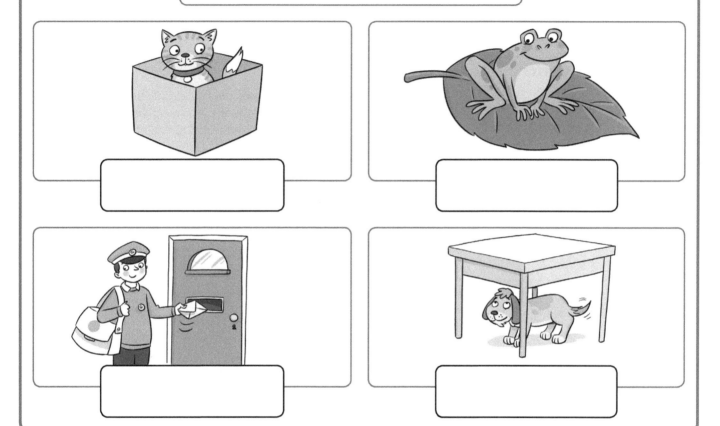

Write a word for the picture that describes how the animal is hidden.

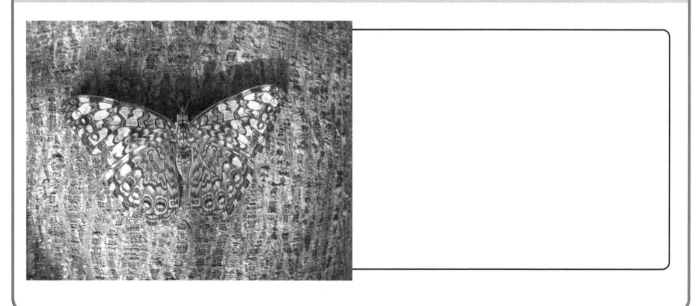

© HarperCollins*Publishers* 2018

Look at Them Go

Book band: Red B

This non-fiction book uses simple mechanics and physics to explain how these devices work: a pull back car, a catapult, a clock, a water blaster, a bike and a hot air balloon.

Practising phonics Phase 3

Warm up: Alien words

- Practise the graphemes children know by reading alien words. Write each of these words on a card and decorate it with an alien: **zear**, **foip**, **shart**, **thairk**.
- Tell children these words are the names of aliens. They are not real words. Show children a word: **zear**.
- Ask them to call out any digraphs or trigraphs: **ear**. Underline the digraphs or trigraphs and dot the sound buttons.
- Ask children to sound out and blend the word.
- **Tip:** Do not encourage children to read the word without blending. Do not spell alien words.

> **Practise the sounds /ar/ /oo/ /ow/ /ear/ /oi/ /er/ /oo/ /ee/ /ur/ /ai/ /air/, tt, bb**

> **Review: /sh/ /th/ /ch/ /z/**

- Introduce the new sounds to practise the Phase 3 sounds in this book.

- Make sure children are confident reading these sounds.
- Use **Look at Them Go: Resource sheet 1** to introduce the focus sounds: **/air/** and **/oi/**. Encourage children to read the phrase aloud to help them remember the sound each grapheme makes and then say the sound as they trace the letters.

Decoding practice

- Practise reading the words on the front page of the book.
- Children complete the final activity on **Look at Them Go: Resource sheet 1**. They read each word, dot and dash it, and finally match it to the correct picture.

Children read

- Tell children to read the book aloud. Encourage them to sound out the words and explore the pictures.
- Listen to children as they read.
- When children have finished reading, ask them to talk with their partner to complete the activity on pages 14–15.

After reading

Developing fluency

- Read the book aloud and ask children to follow in their books.
  - Tell children to join in with you as you read.
  - Hesitate as you read so children can take over reading the next word.
- Tell children what you are thinking as you read so they can see how you make links between the words and the story, for example: *On pages 6 and 7, I look at the labels to help me understand the sentences. These labels show me the cogs and gears.* Children read the labels on another page and work out what information they are giving.
- Read the book with expression and ask children to have a go at reading with expression to a partner.

Comprehension

- Ask children to talk to their partner about their favourite explanation. Take feedback.

- Each page tells us about how something works. Choose an object and ask children to use the words and pictures to help you explain how it works. Write additional labels together.
- Ask children to use the book to help them label the picture on **Look at Them Go: Resource sheet 2**.

Extending vocabulary

Sequencing

- Look through the book with children and model adding sequencing words and phrases to each explanation. For example: *First push the lever down, then the ball pops off!*
- Work together to use **first**, **next**, **after that** and **finally** to sequence the explanations. Add extra description or more technical words to the explanations.
- Children add sequencing words to retell the instructions on **Look at Them Go: Resource sheet 2**.

Reading for pleasure

The Marvelous Thing That Came from a Spring Gilbert Ford

How Do Toys Work? Joanna Brundle

National Geographic Little Kids First Big Book of Things That Go Karen de Seve

© HarperCollins*Publishers* 2018

Look at Them Go: Resource sheet 1
Phonic focus: /air/ and /oi/

Name: _____

Mark the sound buttons. Find the digraphs and trigraphs in the words and underline them.

/air/ a pair of chairs   /oi/ a coin in soil

Match the words to the pictures.

oil lair coil boil join stairs hair foil

Look at Them Go: Resource sheet 2
Comprehension and Vocabulary

Name: _____

Label the diagram. Use the book and the word bank to help you.

| car   gear   cog |

Number the instructions from 1 to 3.

☐ Pull the car back.

☐ It zooms off.

☐ The coil gets tight.

Use the sequencing words from the word bank to improve the instructions.

| Then   Finally   First |

_____ pull the car back.

_____ the coil gets tight.

_____ it zooms off.

Support for Yellow books
Introduction

Pupil partner practice versus feedback
- Pupil partner practice benefits every child.
- Every child talks and clarifies their learning.
- Teacher controls the type of feedback and who gives it.
- Pupils are less passive: every child is involved, not just children with their hands up.

Source: Shirley Clarke *Active Learning Through Formative Assessment* 2008

- Make sure all children practise reading with a partner.
- Teach children how to be a good partner. Demonstrate listening to someone else when they talk and responding to what they say.
- When you ask a question, ensure all children talk it over with their partner.
- Give children adequate time for practice/talk. Use this time to circulate and assess children's learning.

Yellow Link to Phase 4

	New	Review
Sounds	adjacent consonants with short vowel sounds, e.g. block, chest, sprint	ai, ee, igh, oa, oo, *oo*, ar, or, ur, ow, oi, ear, air, ure, er + double letters (These graphemes are from Red B and will need extra practice.)
High frequency words	went, it's, from, children, just, help	an, as, it, in, am, at, dad, can, get, up, not, mum, him, had, dog, on, back, but, big, if, off, and, this, with, that, then, them, yes, will, for, now, down, see, look, too
Common exception words	have, like, little, when, out, what, said, house, here, once, ask, so, do, some, come, were, there, one	was, you, we, my, they, are, put, push, I, the, go, to, into

(See pages 22–23 *How to teach common exception words* for an example lesson plan.)

Reading multi-syllabic words

Children will read words with two or more syllables from Red A onwards. This is a great way of embedding phonic knowledge. Reading multi-syllabic words with ease is crucial to developing fluency.

*Teaching two-syllable words: **desktop***
- Bend the card so only the first syllable is showing: **desk**.
- Find the digraph. Dot and underline. Ask children to read: **desk**.
- Display the second syllable: **top**. Dot and underline as needed.
- Show children the whole word: **desktop**. Ask them to blend each part: **desk/top**. Say the word: *desktop*.
- Always ensure children understand the meaning of each word they read.

© HarperCollins*Publishers* 2018

What to teach while reading Yellow books

Support for comprehension and language activities at Yellow

By now children can read all the consonants, short vowel sounds and the long vowel graphemes: ai, ee, igh, oa, oo, *oo*, ar, or, ur, ow, oi, ear, air, ure, er. They should be taught to segment words to spell using these graphemes.

When children are writing, encourage them to use the graphemes they know to spell words. This means the words will be phonetically plausible but not always accurately spelt. For example, children might write **draw** as *dror* or **happy** as *happee*.

When children learn to read the alternate vowel graphemes they can begin to make more accurate choices in their spellings. For now, it is essential that children feel they can write any word they wish using the graphemes they are familiar with, as this will ensure they feel successful when writing.

What to teach while reading Yellow books

Phonics: Getting Ready for Blue

Children will be able to move on to the Blue reading books with Phase 4 graphemes when they are able to read the graphemes in the box below with adjacent consonants and blend them into words with confidence.

> ai, ee, igh, oa, oo, *oo*, ar, or, ur, ow, oi, ear, air, ure, er

They should be able to read the following words with confidence:

> green   spoon   flight   clear   sprain   churn   boast   spoil   burst

Use the assessments to discover which Phase 4 graphemes from Yellow books children find tricky and review them. Teach plenty of multi-syllabic words with short vowel sounds and adjacent graphemes, such as:

> windmill   terrific   planet   object   handstand

For each book use the:
- phonic warm up to reinforce blending skills
- phonic activities to practise reading graphemes and words
- phonic activity sheet to practise the focus grapheme for the book you are reading.

Use the assessments (pages 26–34) to ensure children are reading books of the correct band. Regular assessments provide a clear record of pupil progress and ensure children move on to the next band as soon as they are ready.

Informal assessment

Children sometimes make sudden progress and are ready to move on to the next book band before your next regular assessment. If you think a child is ready to move bands between your regular assessment dates, do an informal assessment with a book from the next band.
- Ask the child to read the first four pages.
- Check they are reading at 90% fluency (decoding no more than one word in ten).
- Ask a couple of very simple questions to check basic understanding.
- Ask the child if they feel confident at this band.

148   © HarperCollins*Publishers* 2018

The Best Vest Quest

Book band: Yellow

This is a humorous story about a king on a quest for the perfect vest to wear.

Practising phonics Phase 4

Warm up: Reading words with consonant blends: spl, ft, nd, scr, fr, dr

- Write these words on cards: **splash**, **drift**, **sand**, **scrap**, **from**. Show children a card: **splash**.
- Ask children to look for the digraph in the word and draw a line beneath it: **/sh/**.
- Draw children's attention to the adjacent consonants. Practise blending them: **s/p/l**.
- Ask children to read each sound and blend the word. Ensure they understand what each word means.
- Repeat for the other words.

> **New: consonant blends to practise in this book**
> st, spl, ft, sm, fr, nd, nt, sn, scr

> **Review:** /oo/ /er/ /ar/ /or/ /igh/ /oo/

- Introduce the new sounds to practise the Phase 4 sounds in this book.
- Make sure children are confident reading these sounds.
- Use **The Best Vest Quest: Resource sheet 1** to add sound buttons and underline digraphs.

Decoding practice

- Practise reading the words on the front page of the book.
- Ask children to complete the final activity on **The Best Vest Quest: Resource sheet 1**. Tell them to read the words and match them to the pictures.

Children read

- Tell children to read the book aloud. Encourage them to sound out the words and explore the pictures.
- Listen to children as they read.
- When children have finished reading, ask them to turn to pages 14–15 and discuss them with their partner.

After reading

Developing fluency

- Read the book aloud and ask children to follow in their books.
  - Tell children to join in with you as you read.
  - Hesitate as you read so children can take over reading the next word.
- Tell children what you are thinking as you read so they can see how you make links between the words and the story, for example: *When I read 'The next vest was as soft as a kitten', I can imagine what the vest feels like. Let's all stroke the vest and say, 'Oh, as soft as a kitten!'*
- Read the book with expression and ask children to have a go at reading with expression to a partner.

Comprehension

- Ask children to talk to their partner about the story. Why is the story funny? Take feedback.
- Explain to children why King Chester wanted to replace the first vest. Show children how you find the evidence in the text: *It says the vest 'had a rip and a food splash'.*
- Ask children to find out why each subsequent vest was wrong. Encourage them to work with their partner to find the evidence in the text.
- Use **The Best Vest Quest: Resource sheet 2** to link the description of each vest to its picture. Can children work out which vest King Chester decides is the best vest after all?

Extending vocabulary

- Look at the pages where King Chester has found a vest that is 'as soft as a kitten'. Ask children to read and find out what was wrong with that vest. Take feedback.
- Ask children to discuss why the vest might smell horrid. Take feedback.
- Tell children they are going to describe the horrid smelling vest. Read the words: **stinks**, **reeks**, **whiffs**, **pongs**, **musty**.
- Ask children to help you decide which word they think is the smelliest. Ask children to choose the best word to describe the vest on **The Best Vest Quest: Resource sheet 2**.

Reading for pleasure

How to Catch a Star Oliver Jeffers

The Princess Knight Cornelia Funke

The Smartest Giant in Town Julia Donaldson and Axel Scheffler

The Knight Who Wouldn't Fight Helen Docherty and Thomas Docherty

Sam and Dave Dig a Hole Mac Barnett and Jon Klassen

Quest Aaron Becker

© HarperCollins*Publishers* 2018

The Best Vest Quest: Resource sheet 1
Phonic focus: Adjacent consonants with short vowel sounds

Name: _____

Mark the sound buttons. Find the digraphs in the words and underline them.

snug   quest   soft   drip   splash   crunch

Read the words. Draw lines to match the words to the pictures.

vest

smell

scrub

crab

nest

plum

150   Yellow: The Best Vest Quest   © HarperCollins*Publishers* 2018

The Best Vest Quest: Resource sheet 2
Comprehension (Recalling) and Vocabulary

Name: _____

Read the sentences. Draw a line to match them to the vests.

This vest is as soft as a kitten.

This vest is too hard!

This is a tight pink vest.

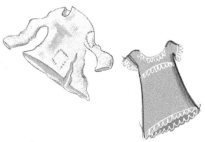

This vest has a rip and a food splash.

Which vest did Chester end up with?

What other words mean 'smells bad'? For example: stinks, reeks, whiffs, pongs, is musty. Write a sentence to describe the vest.

What does the vest smell like?

The vest …

From the Top

Book band: Yellow

This non-fiction book takes you on a journey around the world, looking down from high places, buildings and objects.

Practising phonics Phase 4

Warm up: Alien words
- Practise the graphemes children know by reading alien words.
- Write each of these words on a card and decorate it with an alien: **grat**, **blim**, **homp**, **spuff**, **frem**.
- Tell children these words are the names of aliens. They are not real words.
- Show children a word: **spuff**.
- Ask them to call out any digraphs: /ff/. Underline the digraph and dot the sound buttons.
- Ask children to sound out and blend the word.
- **Tip:** Do not encourage children to read the word without blending. Do not spell alien words.

> **New: consonant blends to practise in this book**
> fr, nd, sp, gr, spr, st, bl, fl, cl

> **Review:** /ee/ /igh/ /oa/ /oo/ /ar/ /ow/ /er/

- Introduce the new sounds to practise the Phase 4 sounds in this book.
- Make sure children are confident reading these sounds.
- Use **From the Top: Resource sheet 1** to add sound buttons and underline digraphs.

Decoding practice
- Practise reading the words on the front page of the book.
- Ask children to complete the final activity on **From the Top: Resource sheet 1**. Tell them to read the words and match them to the pictures.

Children read
- Tell children to read the book aloud. Encourage them to sound out the words and explore the pictures.
- Listen to children as they read.
- When children have finished reading, ask them to turn to pages 14–15 and discuss them with their partner.

After reading

Developing fluency
- Read the book aloud and ask children to follow in their books.
  - Tell children to join in with you as you read.
  - Hesitate as you read so children can take over reading the next word.
- Tell children what you are thinking as you read so they can see how you make links between the words and the story, for example: *When I read 'From this balloon trip in Kenya, you can spot ...', I know that this is about what you can see when you are floating above the animals on safari. It makes me think how amazing it would be to silently float above leopards and lions and giraffes.*
- Read the book with expression and ask children to have a go at reading with expression to a partner.

Comprehension
- Ask children to talk to their partner about the places in the book. Have they ever been up high and looked down? What can they see from their window at home? Take feedback.
- Write a list of things children might see from a bedroom window or from a local viewpoint. Explore how things look different when you are up high.

Extending vocabulary
Synonyms for high
- Ask children to read the word **high** on page 12. Ask: *What other things could be high up?* Take feedback.
- Tell children there are other words that they could use instead of high: **towering**, **soaring**, **tall**, **mountainous**, **steep**.
- Practise saying a short sentence with children using the new words: *The cliff was **towering** above the river. The balloon was **soaring** above the savannah.*
- Ask children to look at each picture and decide which word best describes the height. Ask children to use another word for high to describe the image on **From the Top: Resource sheet 2**.

Reading for pleasure

Iggy Peck, Architect Andrea Beaty and David Roberts
Maps Aleksandra Mizielińska and Daniel Mizieliński
Children's Picture Atlas Ruth Brocklehurst
Look Inside Our World Emily Bone

Hello, is this Planet Earth? Tim Peake
Architecture According to Pigeons Speck Lee Tailfeather
The Magic Bed John Burningham

From the Top: Resource sheet 1
Phonic focus: Adjacent consonants with short vowel sounds

Name: _____

Mark the sound buttons. Find the digraphs in the words and underline them.

| plot | dust | sprint | block | grand | speck |

Read the words. Draw lines to match the words to the pictures.

windmill

brick

tent

spots

hand

clock

© HarperCollins*Publishers* 2018   Yellow: From the Top   153

From the Top: Resource sheet 2
Comprehension (Connecting) and Vocabulary

Name: _____

Talk about the things you can see up high at home or in the local area. Draw and label what you can see. Use the word bank if needed.

**garden   rooftops   river   chairs
bench   car   road   lamp post**

Choose the best synonym for 'high' to describe the picture: towering, soaring, tall, mountainous, steep.

In the Frog Bog

Book band: Yellow

This is a story about Little Frog, who doesn't fit in. He has to visit lots of other frogs until he finds some who accept him just as he is.

Practising phonics Phase 4

Warm up: Reading two-syllable words
- Write these words on cards: **farmyard, boatyard, sandbank, garden, racket**. Bend the card over to show one syllable: **farm**.
- Ask children to identify any digraphs and underline them: **/ar/**. Ask them to read the sounds and blend.
- Repeat for the second syllable: **yard**.
- Show the whole word. Ask children to read each syllable **farm/yard** and then read the whole word: **farmyard**. Ensure children understand the meaning of each word they read.

> **New: consonant blends to practise in this book**
> **spl, pl, st, mp, nd, fr, gr**

> **Review: /ee/ /oa/ /igh/ /ar/ /oi/ /ow/ /or/ /ur/**

- Introduce the new sounds to practise the Phase 4 sounds in this book.
- Make sure children are confident reading these sounds.
- Use **In the Frog Bog: Resource sheet 1** to add sound buttons and underline digraphs.

Decoding practice
- Practise reading the words on the front page of the book.
- Ask children to complete the final activity on **In the Frog Bog: Resource sheet 1**. Tell them to read the words and match them to the pictures.

Children read
- Tell children to read the book aloud. Encourage them to sound out the words and explore the pictures.
- Listen to children as they read.
- When children have finished reading, ask them to turn to pages 14–15 and discuss them with their partner.

After reading

Developing fluency
- Read the book aloud and ask children to follow in their books.
  - Tell children to join in with you as you read.
  - Hesitate as you read so children can take over reading the next word.
- Tell children what you are thinking as you read so they can see how you make links between the words and the story, for example: *When I read 'The farmyard frogs yell, "Stop that racket!"', I think the frogs are really cross so I'm going to make my voice sound loud and cross.* Ask children to practise saying 'Stop that racket!' to their partner with feeling. Can they make their voices sound cross?
- Read the book with expression and ask children to have a go at reading with expression to a partner.

Comprehension
- Children talk about what happens to Little Frog. Have they ever felt left out? Take feedback.
- Talk about how Little Frog might be feeling at different points of the story.
- Expand children's answers to include more ambitious vocabulary – he wasn't just sad, he was: **downcast, miserable, in despair, gloomy**.
- Contrast this with his feelings when he is accepted. Now he isn't just happy, he's: **over the moon, dancing for joy, full of glee** and so on.
- Ask children to look at the pictures of Little Frog on **In the Frog Bog: Resource sheet 2** and write what he is feeling in the thought bubbles.

Extending vocabulary
- Make a list of verbs describing how frogs move: **hop, leap, bound, jump, spring, leapfrog**.
- Help children understand what each action looks like by demonstrating or using a contextualising sentence.
- In the final activity on **In the Frog Bog: Resource sheet 2**, ask children to use an accurate verb in a sentence to describe how Little Frog is moving.

Reading for pleasure

The Little White Owl Tracey Corderoy and Jane Chapman
Odd Dog Out Rob Biddulph
This Book Belongs to Aye-Aye Richard Byrne
Tyrannosaurus Drip Julia Donaldson and David Roberts
Beegu Alexis Deacon

Not All Princesses Dress in Pink Jane Yolen and Heidi E.Y. Stemple
Yuck! That's Not a Monster! Angela McAllister and Alison Edgson
This is Our House Michael Rosen and Bob Graham

© HarperCollins*Publishers* 2018

In the Frog Bog: Resource sheet 1
Phonic focus: Adjacent consonants with short vowel sounds

Name: _____

Mark the sound buttons. Find the digraphs in the words and underline them.

best   splat   stop   gruff   crest   stiff

Read the words. Draw lines to match the words to the pictures.

frog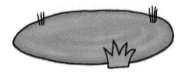

sand

twig

jump

pond

shelf

In the Frog Bog: Resource sheet 2
Comprehension (Character) and Vocabulary

Name: _____

Talk about Little Frog's feelings. Write what he feels in the thought bubbles.

Write a sentence using accurate verbs to show how Little Frog jumps.

Little Frog _____

Stunt Jets

Book band: Yellow

This is a non-fiction book that gives instructions about how to make paper stunt jets.

Practising phonics Phase 4

Warm up: High frequency words

- Write these words on cards: **went**, **it's**, **from**, **children**, **just**, **help**.
- Ask children to help you put sound buttons and mark any digraphs on the words.
- Ask children to read the words independently: put your finger underneath each sound so they know which letter to read.

> **New: consonant blends to practise in this book**
> **ft, nd, pr, st, nt, fl, sw, sp, tw, dr, gr**

> **Review: /ee/ /oo/ /ow/ /oo/ /ur/ /ar/ /air/**

- Introduce the new sounds to practise the Phase 4 sounds in this book.
- Make sure children are confident reading these sounds.

- Use **Stunt Jets: Resource sheet 1** to add sound buttons and underline digraphs.

Decoding practice

- Practise reading the words on the front page of the book.
- Ask children to complete the final activity on **Stunt Jets: Resource sheet 1**. Tell them to read the words and match them to the pictures.

Children read

- Tell children to read the book aloud. Encourage them to sound out the words and explore the pictures.
- Listen to children as they read.
- When children have finished reading, ask them to turn to pages 14–15 and discuss them with their partner.

After reading

Developing fluency

- Read the book aloud and ask children to follow in their books.
  - Tell children to join in with you as you read.
  - Hesitate as you read so children can take over reading the next word.
- Tell children what you are thinking as you read so they can see how you make links between the words and the story, for example: *When I read 'Can you get the jets in?', I know it is a question because the sentence starts with 'Can' and ends with a question mark. When I read it, I am going to say the last word a bit differently so that you know it is a question.* Ask children to read the question with appropriate intonation.
- Read the book with expression and ask children to have a go at reading with expression to a partner.

Comprehension

- Ask children to talk to their partner about the book. Have they ever made a paper aeroplane? Would they like to make one?

- Model following the instructions to make a jet. Show children how you refer to the words, labels and pictures to help you make the jet.
- Ask children to choose one of the jets and follow the instructions to make it with their partner.
- Ask children to put the instructions in order on **Stunt Jets: Resource sheet 2**. Then they can use the words in the word bank to label the diagram of the griffin jet.

Extending vocabulary

Synonyms for speed

- Ask children to talk to their partner about words to describe how fast a jet might go. Take feedback.
- Make a list of words to describe movement: **dart**, **drift**, **buzz**, **zoom**, **dash**, **bolt**, **plod**.
- Use **Stunt Jets: Resource sheet 2** to put the words in order from slowest to fastest. Remind children that there is no perfect order for the words.

Reading for pleasure

Zog and the Flying Doctors Julia Donaldson and Axel Scheffler

Planes and Rockets and Things That Fly Richard Scarry

How to Catch a Star Oliver Jeffers

Q Pootle 5 Nick Butterworth

Tuesday David Wiesner

Blue Michael Rosen and Michael Foreman

The Flying Girl: How Aida de Acosta Learned to Soar Margarita Engle and Sara Palacios

Rosie Revere, Engineer Andrea Beaty and David Roberts

158

© HarperCollins*Publishers* 2018

Stunt Jets: Resource sheet 1
Phonic focus: Adjacent consonants with short vowel sounds

Name: _____

Mark the sound buttons. Find the digraphs in the words and underline them.

lift   swift   bend   flatten   stunt   spot

Read the words. Draw lines to match the words to the pictures.

spin

clap

press

dress

drink

trunk

Stunt Jets: Resource sheet 2
Comprehension (Sequencing) and Vocabulary

Name: _____

Label the jet. Number the instructions 1 to 4.

A griffin jet

wing   tail   tip

☐ Turn the top of the sheet.

☐ Can it dart and drift?

☐ Bend a sheet like this.

☐ Next bend the bottom.

Put the words in order from slowest to fastest.

drift   dash   bolt   plod

_____

The Foolish, Timid Rabbit

Book band: Yellow

This is a traditional tale set in India about a rabbit who hears a loud crash and thinks the world is going to end!

Practising phonics Phase 4

Warm up: Reading words with the digraphs: bb, tt, ck, sh

- Write these words on cards: **rabbit**, **matter**, **crack**, **crash**. Show children a card: **rabbit**.
- Ask children to look for the digraph in the word (two letters that make one sound).
- Draw a dot beneath each sound and a line beneath the digraph: **/bb/**. Remind children that this shows two letters are making one sound.
- Ask children to read each sound and blend the word.
- Repeat for the other words.

> **New: consonant blends to practise in this book
> cr, st, sp, sn, spl, nt, mp, pl, sk**

> **Review: /oo/ /oo/ /ear/ /ar/ /er/**

- Introduce the new sounds to practise the Phase 4 sounds in this book.

- Make sure children are confident reading these sounds.
- Use **The Foolish, Timid Rabbit: Resource sheet 1** to add sound buttons and underline digraphs.

Decoding practice

- Practise reading the words on the front page of the book.
- Ask children to complete the final activity on **The Foolish, Timid Rabbit: Resource sheet 1**. Tell them to read the words and match them to the pictures.

Children read

- Tell children to read the book aloud. Encourage them to sound out the words and explore the pictures.
- Listen to children as they read.
- When children have finished reading, ask them to turn to pages 14–15 and discuss them with their partner.

After reading

Developing fluency

- Read the book aloud and ask children to follow in their books.
  - Tell children to join in with you as you read.
  - Hesitate as you read so children can take over reading the next word.
- Tell children what you are thinking as you read so they can see how you make links between the words and the story, for example: *When I read 'Then Thumper went red', I know that Thumper realises he has made a big mistake and is embarrassed. Can you show me an embarrassed face?*
- Read the book with expression and ask children to have a go at reading with expression to a partner.

Comprehension

- Ask children to talk to their partner about the story. Do they know any other stories with characters that make mistakes? Take feedback.

- Show children the story map on **The Foolish, Timid Rabbit: Resource sheet 2**. Retell the story together.
- Ask children to use the story map to help them retell the story to their partner. They can add words/labels to the map if they wish.

Extending vocabulary

- Read the sentence from page 2: 'Thumper shook with fear.' Ask children to recall why Thumper was scared. Take feedback.
- Together make a list of words to describe Thumper's feelings. Include some more challenging words such as: **dismayed**, **rotten**, **mean**. Make sure children understand the meaning of these words.
- Ask children to show you what the emotions look like with their faces and bodies. Say: *Show me scared. Show me terrified*, and so on.
- Ask children to choose the best words to describe Thumper on **The Foolish, Timid Rabbit: Resource sheet 2**.

Reading for pleasure

Ladybird Tales: Chicken Licken Vera Southgate

The Rabbit Problem Emily Gravett

The Hare and the Tortoise Brian Wildsmith

Because of an Acorn Lola M. Schaefer, Adam Schaefer and Frann Preston-Gannon

Greatest Animal Stories chosen by Michael Morpurgo

© HarperCollins*Publishers* 2018

The Foolish, Timid Rabbit: Resource sheet 1
Phonic focus: Adjacent consonants with short vowel sounds

Name: _____

Mark the sound buttons. Find the digraphs in the words and underline them.

| sped | split | must | crash | stomp | crisp |

Read the words. Draw lines to match the words to the pictures.

crack

stop

splash

tank

truck

pram

The Foolish, Timid Rabbit: Resource sheet 2
Comprehension (Retell) and Vocabulary

Name: _____

Use the story map to retell the story with your partner. Add labels to the story map to help you remember details.

Describe how Thumper is feeling.

© HarperCollins*Publishers* 2018 · Yellow: The Foolish, Timid Rabbit

How the Ear Can Hear

Book band: Yellow

This is a non-fiction book that explores interesting facts about the ear.

Practising phonics Phase 4

Warm up: Countdown

- Write these words on cards: **trip, stamp, splat, scrunch, bump, still, crack, drum, stick, help, fact.**
- Put a timer on for one minute.
- Challenge children to read as many words as they can in one minute.

> **New: consonant blends to practise in this book**
> **lp, mp, spl, scr, st, cr, dr, ct, lf**

> **Review: /ee/ /igh/ /oa/ /oo/ /ar/ /ow/ /er/**

- Introduce the new sounds to practise the Phase 4 sounds in this book.
- Make sure children are confident reading these sounds.

- Use **How the Ear Can Hear: Resource sheet 1** to add sound buttons and underline digraphs.

Decoding practice

- Practise reading the words on the front page of the book.
- Ask children to complete the final activity on **How the Ear Can Hear: Resource sheet 1**. Tell them to read the words and match them to the pictures.

Children read

- Tell children to read the book aloud. Encourage them to sound out the words and explore the pictures.
- Listen to children as they read.
- When children have finished reading, ask them to turn to pages 14–15 and discuss them with their partner.

After reading

Developing fluency

- Read the book aloud and ask children to follow in their books.
  - Tell children to join in with you as you read.
  - Hesitate as you read so children can take over reading the next word.
- Tell children what you are thinking as you read so they can see how you make links between the words and the story, for example: *When I read 'Ears have 17,000 hairs in them!', I am really surprised. I didn't know ears had hairs in them at all! I am going to read it to show surprise.* Ask children to read 'Ears have 17,000 hairs in them!' with feeling.
- Read the book with expression and ask children to have a go at reading with expression to a partner.

Comprehension

- Ask children to talk to their partner about the book. What facts surprised them? Take feedback.

- Ask children to look at the diagram of the ear on page 6. Ask children to read the labels. Check children understand each label.
- Model using the information on the page to complete one label for the diagram of an ear on **How the Ear Can Hear: Resource sheet 2**.
- Ask children to use the book to help them complete the diagram.

Extending vocabulary

- Ask children to talk to their partner about the sounds they hear around them every day. Take feedback.
- Work together to categorise the types of sounds children hear. Start with **quiet** and **loud** and move to more nuanced descriptions such as: **buzzing, hissing, rumbling, sudden, deafening** and so on.
- Ask children to use these words to describe the sounds the objects make on **How the Ear Can Hear: Resource sheet 2**.

Reading for pleasure

What the Ladybird Heard Julia Donaldson and Lydia Monks

What the Jackdaw Saw Julia Donaldson and Nick Sharratt

Listen, Listen Phillis Gershator and Alison Jay

Tanka Tanka Skunk! Steve Webb

Can You Hear the Sea? Judy Cumberbatch

Lullabyhullaballoo Mick Inkpen

All Join In Quentin Blake

164

© HarperCollins*Publishers* 2018

How the Ear Can Hear: Resource sheet 1
Phonic focus: Adjacent consonants with short vowel sounds

Name: _____

Mark the sound buttons. Find the digraphs in the words and underline them.

fact   bump   still   help   plot   splosh

Read the words. Draw lines to match the words to the pictures.

drum

stamp

flat fish

clam

flag

chest

How the Ear Can Hear: Resource sheet 2
Comprehension (Recall) and Vocabulary

Name: _____

Say the phoneme. Label the picture. Use page 6 of the Big Cat book to find the information. Trace the grapheme.

Parts of the ear

ear   ear canal   eardrum

Describe the sounds the objects make.

166   Yellow: How the Ear Can Hear   © HarperCollinsPublishers 2018

Letters and Sounds grapheme charts

Phases 2–3

s	t	p	n	m	d	g	c	r	h	f	l
ss							k / ck			ff	ll
j	v	w	x	y	z	qu	th	ch	sh	ng	nk
					zz						
a	**e**	**i**	**o**	**u**	**ai** sail in the rain	**ee** queen bee	**igh** night light	**oa** boat	**oo** a cool pool	**oo** look in the book	**ar** park the car
or torn shorts	**ur** turns	**ow** How now, Wow Cow!	**oi** a coin in soil	**ear** my ears can hear	**air** a pair of chairs	**ure** a sure cure					
	er power shower										

© HarperCollins*Publishers* 2018

Letters and Sounds grapheme charts

Phases 2–5

Grapheme	Alt. spellings	Grapheme	Alt. spellings	Grapheme	Alt. spellings	Grapheme	Alt. spellings
l	ll, le	**nk**		**ar** (park the car)	a		
f	ff, ph	**ng**		**oo** (look in the book)	ue, ew, u–e, u, ui, ou		
h		**sh**	ch, ti, ci, si, ssi	**oo** (a cool pool)	u, oul		
r	wr	**ch**	tch, t	**oa** (boat)	oe, o–e, ow, o, ou		
c	k, ck, ch, qu, x	**th**		**igh** (night light)	i–e, i, y, ie	**zh** (treasure)	sure, sion, sual, ge
g		**qu**		**ee** (queen bee)	ea, e–e, y, ie, ey, e	**ure** (a sure cure)	ou
d		**z**	zz, se	**ai** (sail in the rain)	ay, a–e, ei, ey, a, eigh	**air** (a pair of chairs)	are, ere
m	mb	**y**		**u** (umbrella)	o, our, o–e	**ear** (my ears can hear)	ere, eer
n	kn, gn	**x**		**o** (octopus)	a	**oi** (a coin in soil)	oy
p		**w**	wh	**i** (ladybird)	y	**ow** (How now, Wow Cow!)	ou
t		**v**	ve	**e** (egg)	ea	**ur** (turns)	er, ir, or, ear
s	ss, c, ce, sc	**j**	g, ge, dge	**a** (apple)		**or** (torn shorts)	aw, au, our, al, augh

168

© HarperCollins*Publishers* 2018

Common exception words

An overview of common exception words in *Big Cat Phonics for Letters and Sounds* in the order they appear

Year	Book Band	Phase in Letters and Sounds	National Curriculum	Letters and Sounds
Reception	Pink A (Chant and Chatter)	2	a is	
	Pink B (Chant and Chatter)	2	a as is of his has	to the no go I into
	Red A and B	3	put pull full push	he she we me be was you they all my her
Year 1	Yellow	4	house here once ask	said have like so do some come were there little one when out what
	Blue	4	school your love our	

Common exception words: when they become decodable

Book Band	Cumulative common exception words	Words now decodable
Pink A	a is	
Pink B	a is as of his has to the no go I into	
Red A and B	of to the no go I into all her by put pull full push are my he she we me be was you they	Red A: a as is his has Red B: her
Yellow	of to the no go I into all by put pull full push are my he she we me be was you they said have like so do some come were there little one when out what house here once ask	
Blue	of to the no go I into all by put pull full push are my he she we me be was you they said have like so do some come were there little one when out what house here once ask school your love our	

© HarperCollins*Publishers* 2018

Focus phonemes in each Pink A – Red A book

The following focus phonemes are explored through the I Spy pages at the end of each book listed below.

Book band	Book	Focus phonemes
Pink A	Book 1 Pat it	s
	Book 2 Pit Pat	a
	Book 3 Sip it	d, n
	Book 4 Map Man	p
	Book 5 Pip Pip Pip	m, i
	Book 6 Tip it	t
Pink B	Book 7 Dig it	o, g
	Book 8 Not a Pot	c, k, ck
	Book 9 Pop Pop Pop!	e, u
	Book 10 Up on Deck	r, h
	Book 11 Mog and Mim	b, f, ff
	Book 12 Bad Luck, Dad	l, ll, ss
Red A	This is My Kit	th, ng, ch
	Zip and Zigzag	j, v
	Big Mud Run	qu, w
	Fantastic Yak	y, x
	In the Fish Tank	sh, nk
	Up in a Rocket	z, zz, ng

Reading for pleasure books

We have developed a list of picture books linked to each *Big Cat Phonics for Letters and Sounds* book. Read these books to your pupils to help them make wider connections so that they can enjoy their reading books even more.

Lilac

Number Fun
Whoosh Around the Mulberry Bush Jan Ormerod and Lindsey Gardiner
My Granny Went to Market: A Round-the-world Counting Rhyme Stella Blackstone and Christopher Corr
Ten Little Pirates Mike Brownlow and Simon Rickerty
Nursery Rhymes Lucy Cousins
Each Peach Pear Plum Janet and Allan Ahlberg

I Spy Nursery Rhymes
Over the Hills and Far Away: A Treasury of Nursery Rhymes from Around the World Elizabeth Hammill
The Great Nursery Rhyme Disaster David Conway and Melanie Williamson
Quentin Blake's Nursery Rhyme Book Quentin Blake
Each Peach Pear Plum Janet and Allan Ahlberg
Tales from Acorn Wood Julia Donaldson and Axel Scheffler
Anno's Counting Book Mitsumasa Anno
The Very Hungry Caterpillar Eric Carle
One Gorilla: A Counting Book Anthony Browne
Have You Seen My Dragon? Steve Light
Tip Tap Went the Crab Tim Hopgood

I Spy Fairytales
Mixed Up Fairy Tales Hilary Robinson and Nick Sharratt
Prince Cinders Babette Cole
Princess Smartypants Babette Cole
Jack and the Baked Beanstalk Colin Stimpson
Very Little Red Riding Hood Teresa Heapy and Sue Heap
The Jolly Postman or Other People's Letters Janet and Allan Ahlberg
The Three Little Wolves and the Big Bad Pig Eugene Trivizas and Helen Oxenbury
The Magic Paintbrush
Little Red Riding Hood
Hansel and Gretel
Cinderella
Goldilocks and the Three Bears
Jack and the Beanstalk

Animal Fun
Dear Zoo Rod Campbell
Brown Bear, Brown Bear, What Do You See? Bill Martin, Jr and Eric Carle
Abigail Catherine Rayner
Animal Ark: Celebrating Our Wild World in Poetry and Pictures Kwame Alexander and Joel Sartore
The Rainforest Grew All Around Susan K. Mitchell
What the Ladybird Heard Julia Donaldson and Lydia Monks
Flip Flap Jungle Axel Scheffler
Hug Jez Alborough
Can You Say it Too? Moo Moo! Sebastien Braun
Blown Away Rob Biddulph
From Head to Toe Eric Carle
Dogs Emily Gravett

Sound Walk
At the Beach Roland Harvey
Busy, Busy World Richard Scarry
Out and About: A First Book of Poems Shirley Hughes
Charlie and Lola: We Honestly Can Look After Your Dog Lauren Child
Handa's Surprise Eileen Browne
Busy, Busy Town Richard Scarry
Shark in the Park! Nick Sharratt
Lucy & Tom At the Seaside Shirley Hughes
Can You Hear the Sea? Judy Cumberbatch and Ken Wilson-Max
Tanka Tanka Skunk! Steve Webb
All Join In Quentin Blake
And the Train goes… William Bee
Noisy Poems Jill Bennett and Nick Sharratt

My Day, Our World
Five Minutes' Peace Jill Murphy
Just Imagine Nick Sharratt and Pippa Goodhart
Can't You Sleep, Little Bear? Martin Waddell and Barbara Firth
Oh, The Places You'll Go! Dr. Seuss
My World, Your World Melanie Walsh

© HarperCollins*Publishers* 2018

Reading for pleasure books

Pink

Pat it
What the Ladybird Heard Julia Donaldson and
   Lydia Monks
Farmer Duck Martin Waddell
Where, Oh Where is Rosie's Chick? Pat Hutchins
A Visit to City Farm Verna Wilkins and Karin Littlewood

Pit Pat
Alfie Weather Shirley Hughes
Rosie's Hat Julia Donaldson
*The Wild Weather Book: Loads of things to do outdoors
   in rain, wind and snow* Fiona Danks and Jo Schofield
Bringing the Rain to Kapiti Plain Verna Aardema and
   Beatriz Vidal

Sip it
How Did That Get in My Lunchbox? Chris Butterworth
*Juliana's Bananas: Where do your bananas come
   from?* Ruth Walton
Eat Your Greens, Goldilocks Steve Smallman and
   Bruno Robert
Tasty Poems Jill Bennett and Nick Sharratt

Map Man
Traction Man is Here Mini Grey
Supertato Sue Hendra
Stuck Oliver Jeffers
Amelia Earhart Ma Isabel Sanchez Vegara
   and Mariadiamantes

Pip Pip Pip
The Elves and the Shoemaker
The Enormous Turnip
The Smartest Giant in Town Julia Donaldson and
   Axel Scheffler
The Lion Inside Rachel Bright and Jim Field
The Crow's Tale Naomi Howarth

Tip it
Tidy Emily Gravett
Recycling Things to Make and Do Emily Bone and
   Leonie Pratt
The Tin Forest Helen Ward and Wayne Anderson
Dinosaurs and All That Rubbish Michael Foreman
Stories for a Fragile Planet Kenneth Steven and
   Jane Ray

Dig it
Eddie's Garden Sarah Garland
Yucky Worms Vivian French
The Curious Garden Peter Brown
The Tiny Seed Eric Carle

Not a Pot
*Captain Flinn and the Pirate Dinosaurs: Missing
   Treasure!* Giles Andreae
The Runaway Dinner Allan Ahlberg
Snail Trail Ruth Brown

Pop Pop Pop!
The Witch with an Itch Helen Baugh
The Most Magnificent Thing Ashley Spires
Ada Twist, Scientist Andrea Beaty

Up on Deck
Mr Gumpy's Outing John Burningham
The River: An Epic Journey to the Sea Patricia Hegarty
Hop Aboard! Here We Go! Richard Scarry
First Book of Ships and Boats Isabel Thomas
Little Tim and the Brave Sea Captain Edward Ardizzone

Mog and Mim
Beegu Alexis Deacon
Man on the Moon Simon Bartram
Q Pootle 5 Nick Butterworth
Toys in Space Mini Grey

Bad Luck, Dad
Bear & Hare Go Fishing Emily Gravett
Fishing with Grandma Susan Avingaq
One Smart Fish Christopher Wormell

Red

This is My Kit
Crafting With Kids Catherine Woram
The Curious Kid's Science Book Asia Citro
Ada Twist, Scientist Andrea Beaty
Gravity Jason Chin

Zip and Zigzag
Shark in the Park! Nick Sharratt
Percy's Bumpy Ride Nick Butterworth
The Park in the Dark Martin Waddell
You Choose Nick Sharratt and Pippa Goodhart

Big Mud Run
*The Wild Weather Book: Loads of things to do outdoors
   in rain, wind and snow* Fiona Danks and Jo Schofield
Ready Steady Mo! Mo Farah
Dinosaur Chase! Benedict Blathwayt
Mud Mary Lyn Ray

Fantastic Yak
Farmer Duck Martin Waddell
The Rainbow Fish Marcus Pfister
Pumpkin Soup Helen Cooper

172   © HarperCollins*Publishers* 2018

Reading for pleasure books

In the Fish Tank
Charlie & Lola: We Honestly Can Look After Your Dog Lauren Child
The Pet Person Jeanne Willis and Tony Ross
How to Look After Your Goldfish David Alderton
The New Puppy Catherine and Laurence Anholt

Up in a Rocket
The Way Back Home Oliver Jeffers
Bob and the Moon Tree Mystery Simon Bartram
Laika the Astronaut Owen Davey

Pink Boat, Pink Car
It Was You, Blue Kangaroo! Emma Chichester Clark
I Want My Hat Back Jon Klassen
Oh No, George! Chris Haughton

A Bee on a Lark
Fox in Socks Dr. Seuss
Pass the Jam, Jim Kaye Umansky
Giant Jelly Jaws and the Pirates Helen Baugh and Ben Mantle
A Squash and a Squeeze Julia Donaldson and Axel Scheffler

Wow Cow!
Supertato Sue Hendra
Super Stan Matt Robertson
Zippo the Super Hippo Kes Gray

Get Set For Fun
The Den Book Jo Schofield and Fiona Danks
Woodland Adventure Handbook Adam Dove
The Wild Woods Simon James
Stanley's Stick John Hegley

It is Hidden
Neon Leon Jane Clarke
Secrets of Animal Camouflage Carron Brown and Wesley Robins
The Mixed-Up Chameleon Eric Carle

Look at Them Go
The Marvelous Thing That Came from a Spring Gilbert Ford
How Do Toys Work? Joanna Brundle
National Geographic Little Kids First Big Book of Things That Go Karen de Seve

Yellow

The Best Vest Quest
How to Catch a Star Oliver Jeffers
The Princess Knight Cornelia Funke
The Smartest Giant in Town Julia Donaldson and Axel Scheffler
The Knight Who Wouldn't Fight Helen Docherty and Thomas Docherty
Sam and Dave Dig a Hole Mac Barnett and Jon Klassen
Quest Aaron Becker

From the Top
Iggy Peck, Architect Andrea Beaty and David Roberts
Maps Aleksandra Mizieli´nska and Daniel Mizieli´nski
Children's Picture Atlas Ruth Brocklehurst
Look Inside Our World Emily Bone
Hello, is this Planet Earth? Tim Peake
Architecture According to Pigeons Speck Lee Tailfeather
The Magic Bed John Burningham

In the Frog Bog
The Little White Owl Tracey Corderoy and Jane Chapman
Odd Dog Out Rob Biddulph
This Book Belongs to Aye-Aye Richard Byrne
Tyrannosaurus Drip Julia Donaldson and David Roberts
Beegu Alexis Deacon
Not All Princesses Dress in Pink Jane Yolen and Heidi E.Y. Stemple
Yuck! That's Not a Monster! Angela McAllister and Alison Edgson
This is Our House Michael Rosen and Bob Graham

Stunt Jets
Zog and the Flying Doctors Julia Donaldson and Axel Scheffler
Planes and Rockets and Things That Fly Richard Scarry
How to Catch a Star Oliver Jeffers
Q Pootle 5 Nick Butterworth
Tuesday David Wiesner
Blue Michael Rosen and Michael Foreman
The Flying Girl: How Aida de Acosta Learned to Soar Margarita Engle and Sara Palacios
Rosie Revere, Engineer Andrea Beaty and David Roberts

The Foolish, Timid Rabbit
Ladybird Tales: Chicken Licken Vera Southgate
The Rabbit Problem Emily Gravett
The Hare and the Tortoise Brian Wildsmith
Because of an Acorn Lola M. Schaefer, Adam Schaefer and Frann Preston-Gannon
Greatest Animal Stories chosen by Michael Morpurgo

How the Ear Can Hear
What the Ladybird Heard Julia Donaldson and Lydia Monks
What the Jackdaw Saw Julia Donaldson and Nick Sharratt
Listen, Listen Phillis Gershator and Alison Jay
Tanka Tanka Skunk! Steve Webb
Can You Hear the Sea? Judy Cumberbatch
Lullabyhullaballoo Mick Inkpen
All Join In Quentin Blake

© HarperCollins*Publishers* 2018

Nursery Rhymes booklet

Sharing nursery rhymes with children helps them to acquire and develop critical skills for learning to read: phonics, comprehension, language development, a rich vocabulary and finding pleasure in sharing words and pictures.

Nursery rhymes help children to experience rhythm and rhyme and hear the sound structure in words. As children begin to hear the sounds and syllables in words they start to build a foundation for learning to read with phonics.

Many nursery rhymes also contain story features and structures for children to draw on when learning to read and write. These include: characters, scenes, story structures (beginning, middle and end) and sequencing of events. And children also get to explore a rich and interesting vocabulary which is open to them beyond every day conversational talk. Just think about the story features and vocabulary used in nursery rhymes such as *Little Miss Muffet*, *The Grand Old Duke of York* and *Humpty Dumpty*.

Nursery rhymes are also part of a child's heritage and, as with traditional stories and fairy tales, many children's books make reference to them. For example, *Each Peach Pear Plum* and the play on the nursery rhyme *Twinkle Twinkle* in *Alice in Wonderland*: 'Twinkle Twinkle Little Bat, How I wonder what you're at …'. This ensures that children acquire a strong foundation for accessing the canon of children's literature later on.

The great thing about nursery rhymes is that everyone can join in with them so it becomes a sociable activity. And most importantly, they ignite a child's imagination and show that playing with words and images can be fun!

Nursery Rhymes

There Was an Old Woman Who Lived in a Shoe

There was an old woman who lived in a shoe.
She had so many children, she didn't know what to do.
She gave them some broth without any bread;
And whipped them all soundly and put them to bed.

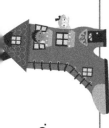

Three Blind Mice

Three blind mice, three blind mice,
See how they run, see how they run,
They all ran after the farmer's wife,
Who cut off their tails with a carving knife,
Did you ever see such a thing in your life,
As three blind mice?

Twinkle Twinkle

Twinkle, twinkle, little star
How I wonder what you are
Up above the world so high
Like a diamond in the sky
Twinkle, twinkle little star
How I wonder what you are

Two Little Dickie Birds

Two little dickie birds sitting on a wall
One named Peter, one named Paul
Fly away Peter, fly away Paul
Come back Peter, come back Paul

Wee Willie Winkie

Wee Willie Winkie runs through the town,
Upstairs and downstairs in his nightgown,
Tapping at the window and crying through the lock,
Are all the children in their beds, it's past eight o'clock?

Baa Baa Black Sheep

Baa, baa, black sheep
Have you any wool?
Yes sir, yes sir, three bags full.
One for the master,
And one for the dame,
And one for the little boy
Who lives down the lane.

Five Little Ducks

Five little ducks went swimming one day
Over the hill and far away
Mother duck said, "Quack quack quack quack"
And only four little ducks came back!
Four little ducks went swimming one day
Over the hill and far away
Mother duck said, "Quack quack quack quack"
And only three little ducks came back!
Three little ducks went swimming one day
Over the hill and far away
Mother duck said, "Quack quack quack quack"
And only two little ducks came back!
Two little ducks went swimming one day
Over the hill and far away.
Mother duck said, "Quack quack quack quack"
And only one little duck came back!
One little duck went swimming one day
Over the hill and far away
Mother duck said, "Quack quack quack quack"
And all her five little ducks came back!

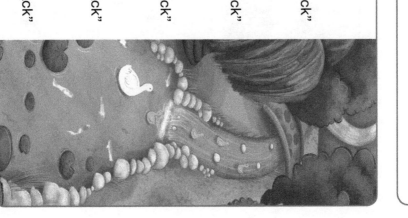

Frère Jacques (Are You Sleeping?)

Frère Jacques, Frère Jacques,
Dormez-vous? Dormez-vous?
Sonnez les matines, sonnez les matines
Ding ding dong, ding ding dong.
Are you sleeping, are you sleeping?
Brother John, Brother John?
Morning bells are ringing, morning bells are ringing
Ding ding dong, ding ding dong.

Girls and Boys Come Out to Play

Girls and boys come out to play
The moon doth shine as bright as day
Leave your supper, and leave your sleep
And join children in the street.
Come with a whoop, and come with a call
Come with a good will or not at all
Up the ladder and down the wall
A penny loaf will serve you all.
Girls and boys come out to play
The moon doth shine as bright as day
Leave your supper, and leave your sleep
And join children in the street.

Here We Go Round the Mulberry Bush

Here we go round the mulberry bush
The mulberry bush, the mulberry bush
Here we go round the mulberry bush
On a cold and frosty morning.

This is the way we wash our face
Wash our face, wash our face
This is the way we wash our face
On a cold and frosty morning

This is the way we brush our teeth
Brush our teeth, brush our teeth
This is the way we brush our teeth
On a cold and frosty morning

This is the way we put on our clothes
Put on our clothes, put on our clothes
This is the way we put on our clothes
On a cold and frosty morning

This is the way we eat our food
Eat our food, eat our food
This is the way we eat our food
On a cold and frosty morning

This is the way we go to school
Go to school, go to school
This is the way we go to school
On a cold and frosty morning

Hey Diddle Diddle

Hey, diddle, diddle,
The cat and the fiddle,
The cow jumped over the moon;
The little dog laughed
To see such fun,
And the dish ran away with the spoon.

Incy Wincy Spider

Incy Wincy spider climbed up the waterspout,
Down came the rain and washed the spider out,
Out came the sun and dried up all the rain,
So Incy Wincy spider climbed up the spout again.

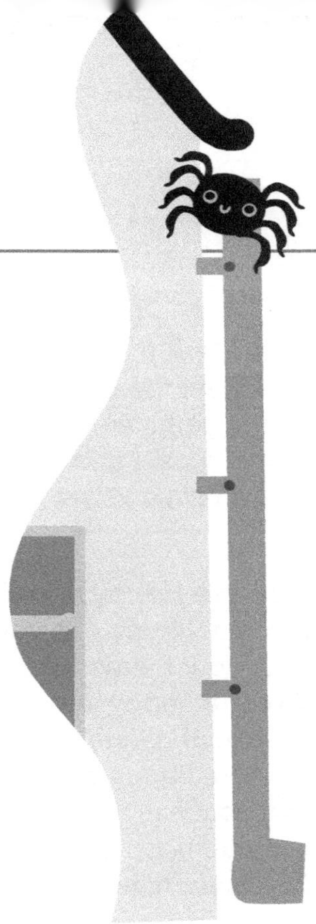

Hot Cross Buns

Hot cross buns!
Hot cross buns!
One a penny, two a penny.
Hot cross buns!
If you have no daughters,
Give them to your sons!
One a penny, two a penny.
Hot cross buns!

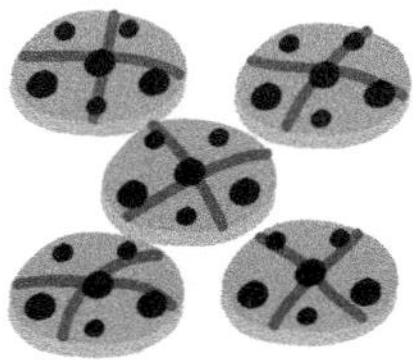

Hush Little Baby – Mockingbird

(please note: change Papa to Mama, Grandpa, etc. if required)

Hush, little baby, don't say a word.
Papa's gonna buy you a mockingbird
And if that mockingbird won't sing,
Papa's gonna buy you a diamond ring
And if that diamond ring turns brass,
Papa's gonna buy you a looking glass
And if that looking glass gets broke,
Papa's gonna buy you a billy goat
And if that billy goat won't pull,
Papa's gonna buy you a cart and bull
And if that cart and bull turn over,
Papa's gonna buy you a dog named Rover
And if that dog named Rover won't bark
Papa's gonna buy you a horse and cart
And if that horse and cart fall down,
You'll still be the sweetest little baby in town.

Hickory Dickory Dock

Hickory Dickory Dock,
The mouse ran up the clock.
The clock struck one,
The mouse ran down!
Hickory Dickory Dock.

Hark Hark the Dogs do Bark

Hark hark the dogs do bark
The beggars are coming to town
Some in rags and some in jags
And one in a velvet gown.

If You're Happy and You Know It

If you're happy and you know it
Clap your hands. *Clap, Clap.*
If you're happy and you know it
Clap your hands. *Clap, Clap.*
If you're happy and you know it
and you really want to show it
If you're happy and you know it
Clap your hands. *Clap, Clap.*

If you're angry and you know it
Stomp your feet. *Stomp, Stomp.*
If you're angry and you know it
Stomp your feet. *Stomp, Stomp.*
If you're angry and you know it
and you really want to show it
If you're angry and you know it
Stomp your feet. *Stomp, Stomp.*

Jack and Jill

Jack and Jill went up the hill.
To fetch a pail of water.
Jack fell down and broke his crown,
And Jill came tumbling after.

Up Jack got, and home did trot,
As fast as he could caper,
He went to bed to mend his head
With vinegar and brown paper.

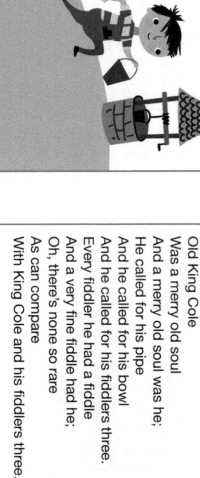

Little Bo Peep

Little Bo Peep has lost her sheep,
And can't tell where to find them;
Leave them alone, and they'll come home,
Bringing their tails behind them.

Little Boy Blue

Little Boy Blue, come blow your horn,
The sheep's in the meadow, the cow's in the corn
Where is the boy who looks after the sheep?
He's under the haystack, fast asleep.

Mary Had a Little Lamb

Mary had a little lamb,
Its fleece was white as snow;
And everywhere that Mary went
The lamb was sure to go.

Mary Mary Quite Contrary

Mary, Mary, quite contrary
How does your garden grow?
With silver bells and cockleshells
And pretty maids all in a row.

Old King Cole

Old King Cole
Was a merry old soul
And a merry old soul was he;
He called for his pipe
And he called for his bowl
And he called for his fiddlers three.
Every fiddler he had a fiddle
And a very fine fiddle had he;
Oh, there's none so rare
As can compare
With King Cole and his fiddlers three.

Old MacDonald Had a Farm

Old MACDONALD had a farm
Old MACDONALD had a farm
E-I-E-I-O
And on his farm he had a cow
And on his farm he had a sheep
E-I-E-I-O
E-I-E-I-O
With a moo moo here
With a baa baa here
And a moo moo there
And a baa baa there
Here a moo, there a moo
Here a baa, there a baa
Everywhere a moo moo
Everywhere a baa baa
Old MacDonald had a farm
Old MacDonald had a farm
E-I-E-I-O
E-I-E-I-O

Repeat with other animals.

One, Two, Three, Four, Five

One, two, three, four, five,
Once I caught a fish alive,
Six, seven, eight, nine, ten,
Then I let it go again.
Why did you let it go?
Because it bit my finger so.
Which finger did it bite?
This little finger on the right.

Pat-a-Cake

Pat-a-cake, pat-a-cake, baker's man.
Bake me a cake as fast as you can,
Pat it and prick it and mark it with B,
And bake it in the oven for baby and me.

Polly put the kettle on

Polly put the kettle on,
Polly put the kettle on,
Polly put the kettle on,
We'll all have tea!

Sukey take it off again,
Sukey take it off again,
Sukey take it off again,
They've all gone away.

Pussy Cat, Pussy Cat

Pussy cat, pussy cat, where have you been?
I've been to London to visit the Queen.
Pussy cat, pussy cat, what did you there?
I frightened a little mouse under her chair.

Ride a Cock Horse

Ride a cock horse to Banbury Cross,
To see a fine lady upon a white horse;
Rings on her fingers and bells on her toes,
She shall have music wherever she goes.

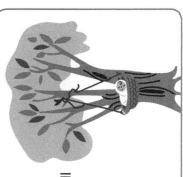

Rock-a-bye Baby

Rock-a-bye baby, in the treetop
When the wind blows, the cradle will rock
When the bough breaks, the cradle will fall
And down will come baby, cradle and all.

Row Row Row Your Boat

Row, row, row your boat,
Gently down the stream,
Merrily, merrily, merrily, merrily,
Life is but a dream.

Rub-a-Dub-Dub

Rub-a-dub-dub,
Three men in a tub.
And who do you think they be?
The butcher,
The baker,
The candlestick-maker!
And all of them going to sea!

Sing a Song of Sixpence

Sing a song of sixpence,
A pocket full of rye,
Four and twenty blackbirds
Baked in a pie.
When the pie was opened
The birds began to sing –
Wasn't that a dainty dish
To set before the king?

The king was in the counting-house
Counting out his money,
The queen was in the parlour
Eating bread and honey,
The maid was in the garden
Hanging out the clothes.
Along came a blackbird
And snipped off her nose.

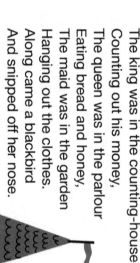

Ten in the Bed

There were ten in the bed and the little one said,
'Roll over, roll over!'
So they all rolled over and one fell out
There were nine in the bed and the little one said,
'Roll over, roll over!'
So they all rolled over and one fell out
There were eight in the bed and the little one said,
'Roll over, roll over!'
So they all rolled over and one fell out
There were seven in the bed and the little one said,
'Roll over, roll over!'
So they all rolled over and one fell out
There were six in the bed and the little one said,
'Roll over, roll over!'
So they all rolled over and one fell out
There were five in the bed and the little one said,
'Roll over, roll over!'
So they all rolled over and one fell out
There were four in the bed and the little one said,
'Roll over, roll over!'
So they all rolled over and one fell out
There were three in the bed and the little one said,
'Roll over, roll over!'
So they all rolled over and one fell out
There were two in the bed and the little one said,
'Roll over, roll over!'
So they all rolled over and one fell out
There was one in the bed and the little one said,
'Good night!'

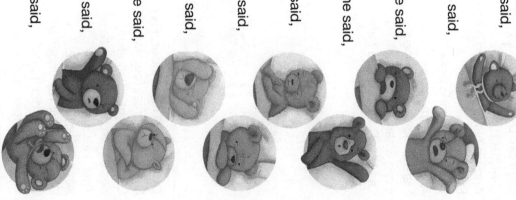

There Was a Crooked Man

There was a crooked man, and he walked a crooked mile,
He found a crooked sixpence against a crooked stile;
He bought a crooked cat which caught a crooked mouse,
And they all lived together in a little crooked house.